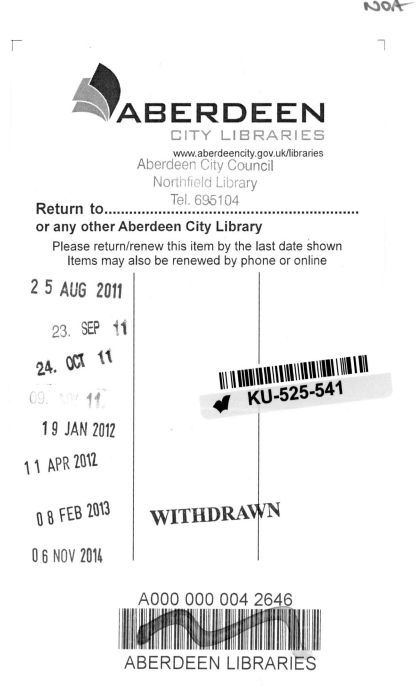

NOA

# ABERDEEN
## CITY LIBRARIES

Possibly the only librarian who got told off herself for talking too much, **Natalie Anderson** decided writing books might be more fun than shelving them—and, boy, is it that! Especially writing romance—it's the realisation of a lifetime dream kick-started by many an afternoon spent devouring Grandma's Mills & Boon® novels…

She lives in New Zealand with her husband and four gorgeous-but-exhausting children. Swing by her website any time—she'd love to hear from you: www.natalie-anderson.com

# NICE GIRLS FINISH LAST

BY
NATALIE ANDERSON

First published in Great Britain 2011
by Mills & Boon, an imprint of Harlequin (UK) Limited,
Eton House, 18-24 Paradise Road, Richmond, Surrey TW9 1SR

© Natalie Anderson 2011

ISBN: 978 0 263 220810

Harlequin (UK) policy is to use papers that are natural, renewable and recyclable products and made from wood grown in sustainable forests. The logging and manufacturing process conform to the legal environmental regulations of the country of origin.

Printed and bound in Great Britain
by CPI Antony Rowe, Chippenham, Wiltshire

**Also by Natalie Anderson:**

DATING AND OTHER DANGERS
THE END OF FAKING IT
WALK ON THE WILD SIDE
UNBUTTONED BY HER MAVERICK BOSS*
CAUGHT ON CAMERA WITH THE CEO*
TO LOVE, HONOUR AND DISOBEY

*Part of the *Hot Under the Collar* duet

**Did you know these are also available as eBooks?
Visit www.millsandboon.co.uk**

For Miss S, aka Rachel, aka Life-Saver—
thanks so much for helping me out!

# CHAPTER ONE

'Coming through!' Lena clapped one hand over her eyes and pushed the changing room door open. She always sang out the warning, giving them time to cover up if they wanted. Some did, most no longer bothered. Eighteen months in the job and they were so used to her being around she might as well be wallpaper. But today she was in and out more than usual, and they were in and out of clothes more than usual, too.

She peeked through her fingers and registered that they were out of their clothes at the moment—but that they'd towels round their waists. Short towels. Dropping her hand from her face, she lifted the heavy bag off her shoulder and started pulling out the contents. 'I've got the next lot—you want them now?'

'Not yet, it's the shower shot,' Ty, the team captain, answered for everyone.

'Oh, okay.' She dropped the handful of shorts and looked up to find a place to leave the bag. And froze. Silently she swivelled her eyeballs left to right and back again and refused to let her reaction show.

Because nineteen nearly naked guys now surrounded her. *Closely* surrounded her.

Lena called on all her internal discipline to keep her focus up on their mischievous faces. The temptation to ogle was always there—how could it not be? They were championship-winning athletes with the megamuscles to prove it and no red-blooded woman could be immune to the urge to admire.

Lena was as red-blooded as any other woman. She just pretended not to be.

She narrowed her gaze because they were all grinning at her and stepping closer still, tightening the circle. Yep, she was in the middle of the men's changing room, in the middle of a rugby scrum. While there might be thousands of women in the world who'd beg to be in that exact position—*sans the towels*—she wasn't one of them.

'What are you doing?' she demanded, affecting a long-suffering big-sister tone.

'We need your help,' Ty answered for them all again, too innocently.

She handed him the bag in the hope he'd step back and take the others with him. 'I've got to go and get the shirts. I'm just getting creases out of a couple of them.'

Her job description included that nebulous sentence 'other duties as required', and this one day of the year that meant playing the part of wardrobe mistress while the Silver Knights endured the photo shoot for their annual calendar.

'We need you to do something else first,' Jimmy, the first five-eighth, spoke up.

'Really? What?'

'The photographer says we have to glisten.'

Lena closed her mouth and took a microsecond to keep cool. Then she asked for clarification. 'Glisten?'

Jimmy nodded and held up a bottle. Baby oil. 'All over the torso.'

'You can rub it on each other.' She bit back an add-on comment about them *liking* grappling each other out there in the mud. She never let sassy snark out in the stadium;

professionally polite was how she played it. Once she got to know the newbies she was friendly in a sisterly way, but, until then, pretty frigid.

'We've got ball shots coming up straight after.' They glanced at each other and smirked. 'We'd lose our grip if we get that oil on our hands. Too slippery.'

Slippery, huh? With balls. Oh, they were appalling today.

Lena might not be interested but she was human and being surrounded by nineteen nearly naked, extremely buff sports stars would make any woman break into a sweat. Lena point-blank refused to sweat but, even so, her temperature slid up a notch. 'Just wash your hands,' she slowly stated the obvious solution.

'It doesn't work.' Ty rubbed the tips of his fingers in her face as if to show how slippery they still were.

'You have to help us,' Max, one of the props, pleaded with puppy-style eyes. 'I mean, we could get the photographer to do it but…' He trailed off.

She knew these ultra-competitive jocks liked to tease. She had their respect. They always listened to her work requests and refrained from the worst of their laddishness around her, but she also knew they urged any new recruit to have a crack at asking her out. It seemed being shot down by her was some kind of initiation ritual for the young bloods. So she never failed to disappoint and said no to everyone. Truthfully, gorgeous as they were, she didn't *want* to date any of them. Driven, elite demigods never prioritised girl-friends, and in her next relationship—which would be years from now anyway—she was totally being the top priority. Not to mention, the only woman. Three was so a crowd.

Besides, it wasn't as if they actually wanted to date *her*. She wasn't some to-die-for babe, it was simply another game for them, not anything to take seriously or be flattered by.

But facing this prank now, she refused to be flustered,

wouldn't blush or giggle or do anything girly. She knew what they were waiting for—the usual clipped brush-off. But they'd just gone a step too far and for once she wasn't going to play the way they expected. They wanted her to rub baby oil all over their torsos?

'Sure, no problem.' She held her hand out for the bottle. 'Who's first?'

Their eyes widened.

'You will?' the guy in front gasped.

Yeah, they'd never have thought she'd say yes. Not when it was her personal policy never to get within two feet of any of them.

'Of course.' She flipped the lid of the bottle and squirted oil into her hand. 'Other duties as required, right?' She stepped up. 'But of course I could sue you guys for sexual harassment....' She paused for effect, then slapped her palm hard on the first broad chest in front of her.

She felt the wince, registered the sudden total silence and suppressed her smile. Yeah, now they were worried.

'It's not like you're the one having to pose almost nude for pictures for people to pin up on their wall,' the puppy-eyed prop managed to wheeze. 'If that's not sexual harassment I don't know what is.'

Lena raised her brows. She squeezed the bottle again. 'That's the price, boys. Fame costs...'

'And we're paying.' The next in line winced as she smacked her oil-slicked hand onto him.

With ruthless efficiency she slapped and swiped oil over the broad bare skin in swift strokes. It took mere moments to get through each in total scary-school-nurse fashion.

'Are you guys ready yet?' The photographer appeared from the tunnel entrance, accompanied by Dion, the stadium's new CEO.

'Almost,' the last one croaked.

'Right,' Lena said briskly, glancing around. They stood silent and wide-eyed. She saw one of them pressing a hand to his chest where she might have slapped him a little *too* hard. She tightly pulled in her mouth to stop from laughing, because despite her efforts to prove the contrary, she *was* human and she had to react to this. But she had to be alone before she could.

'What are you waiting for?' She blasted through the stunned tableau to get to the door she'd come through. 'I'll be back with the shirts in a mo.'

She walked then, her high heels clipping quickly on the concrete floor, because she was a breath away from losing it.

Six paces along the safe corridor she heard it. The riot as they howled. She stopped to listen. Holding her still oil-slicked hands away from her dress, she leaned back on the cool wall, closed her eyes and succumbed to it herself.

Laughter—the husky, thoroughly entertained, wicked laughter that she'd been holding in too tight for too long.

The rogues. The looks on their faces had been priceless and she wished she'd said what she really thought and given them a sassy smack-down. Still, a literal smack or two had been just as satisfying. Her shoulders and ribs shook and her tummy ached, she laughed so hard. Finally she drew in a deep calming breath and opened her eyes.

'Hey!' She flinched, bumping the back of her head on the wall. A stranger was standing right in front of her, closer than the buff rugby boys had been only a few minutes before. She looked at the cool blue eyes boring right through her. Oh, my word. It took less than a second to take in the symmetry of his face, the darkness of his brows above, the curve of the mouth below the vivid, intensely focused eyes...less than a second to clock his height, breadth, strength...less than a second to be overwhelmed by a totally gorgeous stranger…and less than a second for her body to react.

She might have felt a slight warmth in the change room, but her temperature rocket-shot now. A wholly womanly reaction—she burned hot, twitchy, pulsing to life. Which was really, really unusual. She was immune to feeling interest in any of these arrogant athletes, right? She had to be to work here. She pressed harder against the cold concrete, but he didn't step back.

'Been having fun?' It was a drawl. Low, confident, ever so slightly needling.

He was sizing her up. And…she narrowed in on the vibe…disapproving?

Lena's ability to give her customary ice-cold response left the building. Having this random, dead-sexy stranger look at her as if she were the groupie she sure as hell was never going to be kindled a spark of *damn-you* defiance. She looked up at him and suggestively curved her mouth.

'Like you wouldn't believe,' she drawled right back at him.

His eyes narrowed the merest fraction. Oh, yeah, she'd just confirmed his worst suspicions. He did think she was a groupie. So wrong. The new boy needed whipping.

'Should you be down here?' he asked, still not moving out of her personal space. 'I thought this was a restricted area.'

'I guess that depends on who you know,' she said softly, totally unsubtly.

'How many do you know?'

'Oh, I know all of them,' she answered slowly. 'Real well.'

She didn't even have to try to sound husky, her voice just happened that way. The laughter from the change room echoed again—sexually appreciative, masculine amusement.

The stranger's brows flicked. 'And a good time was had by everyone.'

Lena parted her lips a hopefully imperceptible amount—just so she could breathe. She touched the tip of her tongue to them, too, because they were drier than wood dust. She still couldn't break from the prison of his gaze, but he had to be kidding. Did he really think she'd been in there getting an entire rugby team off? Oh, he'd pay for that. She managed another raspy reply. 'You have no idea how good.'

He stepped closer, putting one hand on the wall beside her head. 'Tell me.'

Stunned, her senses flaring, she absorbed his taunting, low invitation. The sudden wicked glint in his eye unlocked some dam hidden deep within her. It burst free, the sensation that had long been buried, picking up the pace of her pulse until it pounded and sent heat steaming through her entire system. Her mad moment of tease in the change room was nothing on the temptation before her now. Her inner imp crossed right over from smart'n'sassy, to out-and-out *wicked.* The urge to shock this one man was irresistible.

'You know, everyone says that it's guys who are visually stimulated,' she said faux thoughtfully. 'That for women arousal is all between the ears or something.'

'And that's not true?'

'No.' She shook her head, but still couldn't break the eye contact. 'We're visual. We *love* to look every bit as much as you do. And a whole room full of beautiful naked men?' she purred. 'I haven't got a brain cell left.'

The corners of his eyes crinkled as his mouth smirked up. 'Did you ever have a brain cell?'

'Well—' she bit her lip and positively batted her lashes at him '—only a couple.'

'And now they're fried?'

'To a crisp,' she whispered breathily.

'The whole team, huh?' Something danced in his eyes.

'Oh, yes,' she sighed. And then she smiled, because she suddenly had it, the way in which she was going to teach this guy the lesson he so badly needed. She reached two inches forward and took hold of his beautifully tailored, no doubt horrifically expensive, jacket. She lifted her face nearer to his as she confirmed breathlessly, 'I had my hands on every single one of them.'

'Did you, now?' He didn't pull back; in fact he leaned closer. Which was just perfect, because she could smooth her hands on him without him really seeing.

Her oily, slippery hands.

'You've no idea, the excitement...' She gazed at him, not realising she'd trailed off. His smile had widened, sparkling up his expression, and the effect was frankly mesmerising.

'You know what?' His voice dropped as he leaned to a mere millimetre away and full out mesmerised her even more. 'I don't believe you.'

She was surprised, and her eyes widened, but she twisted her fingers in the soft, luxurious fabric. 'I never lie.' Not now, she'd learned the lesson hard.

He planted his other hand on the wall beside her. Now she was trapped and the length of his body was a shiver away from the length of hers. Lena was having a time suppressing that shiver. Her breathing spiked as she tried to slow her pulse and pull her brain back from beyond.

She figured he was a new recruit, or a player from another club visiting. He was tall enough, had the shoulders, not to mention the arrogance....

'So you've been kissing all those boys in there?' he asked, his gaze intent and unwavering.

She flicked her brows.

They were nearly nose to nose, his blue-eyed focus still intense, but now blatantly sensual and filled with amusement. It magnified her attraction to him. Bones, muscles, brain—*everything* melted. His expression was different from anything she'd seen in anyone on the team—despite all the invitations. This guy was so focused, so, so intent on her. She could hardly breathe.

'If you'd really been kissing them,' he said, 'I'd see it on your face. But your lipstick is immaculate.'

'Maybe I reapplied.'

'Your lips aren't swollen, your skin isn't flushed, your eyes don't have that gleam.'

His words stoked the insane reactions occurring within her body—her lower belly had become an inferno and it was almost impossible to remain still. The urge to be exceptionally wicked had to be held in place somehow. Except she didn't know how. All she knew was that she was answering him back again. 'I've got a quick recovery. It's necessary, you know, when you take on so many at once. A girl like me has stamina.'

'Oh, you do?' He sounded pleased. 'Then one more isn't going to make much difference, is it?'

She froze. 'One more what?'

Her words may or may not have been audible. Who cared? Because at that moment he moved that shiver closer.

His lips caught hers on the full, claiming complete possession. She didn't even think to stop him. For a moment pure shock immobilised her, sending her strength someplace else. She melted, thankful for the wall behind holding her up.

It had been a hell of a long time between kisses and this was one hell of a kiss. He took total control, first warming her lips with his own, teasing them apart with his tongue, then surging forward and exploring deeper. That brought her back, only not to fight and push him away as she probably should. Oh, no, the only thing she *could* do was open up and kiss him right back. He was absolute masculinity—a wall of heat, strength and solidity that turned her into a malleable woman who'd bend whichever way he wanted.

She heard the growl, felt the shift as he moved closer still so his body pinned hers. His hands cupped her face, holding it up to his, and for a few carnally delightful seconds he seduced the soul out of her. But just as she was really getting into it he broke away, angling so he could look hard at her. His blue eyes blazed.

'Now you have the gleam,' he said, voice thick with satisfaction.

She gasped and started to blast him with some sarky thing on the tip of her tongue—only, before sound even emerged he swooped back and took her tongue with his own. *She* growled then. Oh, he was hot. And bold. And delicious.

She tasted his smile as he switched to a series of soft teasing kisses. His hands slipped to her neck, his fingers stroking downwards, skimming hot sensation over her skin. But her passion ran far deeper than that.

That formerly locked-up dam spilled more heat, spinning it along her veins until anticipation tingled in every cell. Need spiked. She moved, her muscles all fire-fuelled strength. She shivered and pressed her mouth harder to his, hurtling them back to the bruising, blistering, barely controlled hunger of seconds before.

She totally forgot about rubbing the oil on his jacket to pay him back for his smug arrogance and out-of-order assumption. Instead all she could think of was having him closer, harder, heavier against her. She clung as urges rampaged through her. Urges she couldn't suppress. She kissed him—hungry, wild, restless.

*Reckless.*

Her fingers tightened into his jacket, her toes tightened in their shoes, her muscles tightened in her womb. She wanted to clench down on something really hard. And the really hard thing was pushing right against her.

She couldn't have broken free even if she'd wanted to. Some violent force bound them, demanding closer intimacy. More furious, more hungry. She devoured the sensations. Devoured him. Blissfully out of control and utterly abandoned to how good it felt.

Their lips sealed, tongues stroked, locked into a rhythm, deep, rough, outrageously passionate. His hands pressed down her back to shape her waist, and then cupped her bottom, pressing her pelvis harder against his.

It had been for ever since she'd had a physical release. And she'd never been this turned on by a few saucy sentences and a couple of kisses. But this was so much more than kissing. She moaned into his mouth as the uncontrollable fire turned her reason to ash.

She was so tension-filled she couldn't uncurl her fingers, but she pulled her hands apart, jerking his jacket open so she could press her tight, aching breasts against the spectacularly solid wall of his chest. She pulled harder and his jacket slipped partway off his shoulders, half pinning his arms to his sides, but his hands were exactly where she wanted them anyway—gripping her hips, hauling them closer to his in time with every thrust of his tongue.

A door banged. More noise followed—a sudden volume of voices—men's voices.

He released her instantly. Lena crashed back against the wall, hitting cold, hard reality. He stepped up in front of her, his body a barrier so she couldn't be seen from the doorway, a surprisingly protective move. But she didn't stop to say thanks. Not when she'd just blown her rep to smithereens.

Her brain screamed the order. Her body followed it.

She fled.

# CHAPTER TWO

FASTER, faster, faster.

Lena knew exactly how to shortcut through the myriad corridors in the massive complex, so she scurried along them, got to her office, snatched her handbag and was in the ladies' loo before she could gulp the breath her lungs were bursting for.

She gasped when she saw her reflection and thanked all the stars she'd got there without seeing anyone. Her lipstick was a mess, her hair mussed, her mouth huge. As for her eyes, her pupils were so massive and dark she looked as if she were on something. Which she was—lust, hormones, the highest of natural highs, and she'd wanted to ride the wave all the way to the top, not be dropped out halfway to heaven....

Oh, she'd been an idiot.

She scrubbed her hands but could still smell the baby oil. She held a bunch of tissues under the cold tap and pressed them to her lips. It didn't cool them a fraction. She debated whether it was better to reapply lipstick or leave it. Went with reapplying. Not having any would look more unusual. She never went bare at work because she had an image to maintain. Polished, capable, *professional.* The kissy fullness would settle in a few moments, right?

Oh, so stupid, stupid, stupid.

She'd worked so hard to earn respect and a good reputation here and she'd just chucked it. For what?

The kiss of a lifetime. Definitely. But it wasn't worth her job.

Despite her hammering heart and desperate urge to flee the place altogether, she had to go back and implement damage control—sooner rather than later. She swiped her comb through her hair to smooth it, closed her eyes and counted to ten. She'd fix up the last couple of shirts for the team, then deal with the five-car pile-up her life had just become. She fussed with the fabric, getting it perfect while questions spun so fast in her head it was worse than being on some g-force terror ride at a theme park.

Who and how and why was he there? It wasn't the right time in the season for a new recruit and he'd been right about it being a restricted area...so *who*?

And *what* had she been thinking? It was his fault—right? He'd invaded her personal space and made boundary-crossing comments and started the whole explosive episode. *He'd* kissed *her*. She'd been the innocent party...sort of. But her heart knew the truth and her body just wanted *more*.

Seth had shrugged his jacket back up to his shoulders and walked forward as soon as he'd heard the door open. Breathless, his brain obliterated, he had been guided by pure instinct to protect her as best he could.

But in the few seconds it took for the door to bang shut again—with no one having walked through it—she'd gone. Faster than lightning, she'd streaked down the corridor. He didn't chase her; in the split second he saw her turn a corner—she knew exactly the way out of there. He didn't.

So what he had to do was find Dion. Because Dion would be able to tell him who the flamethrower was.

Wow.

He chuckled and wiped the back of his hand over his mouth, checking it. Yeah, a smear of the slick red she wore on her lips coloured his skin. He rubbed again to be sure he was clear, then ran his hands through his hair and exhaled hard, trying to release some of the tension.

As if that were ever going to happen. He was so wound and wired it was a wonder he could even walk. But walk he would—just as soon as some of the blood pumped back out of his pants and up north to his head. It took a few moments—hindered by the fact that all he could think of was that woman with the creamiest skin and the palest green eyes that were totally, *totally* feline. Given the smart-but-pretty dress and heels and make-up she had on, he guessed she worked here, probably PR, given her polished image. Less polished now he'd messed with her....

Yeah, none of these thoughts were helping him recover his control. He forced it, breathing out again and striding forward through the change-room door. 'You in here, Dion?'

Seth stopped a few paces into the room and blinked at the sight. Dion was on the edge of a group of rugby players—all of whom were clad only in white towels, while a few more were posed in one corner of the room. In between the two groupings stood a photographer, camera in front of his face as he issued instructions and click, click, clicked.

'Hey, Seth, glad you could make it.' Dion had recently stepped in as CEO for the stadium. He was another property-development addict, and his new diversion was perfect timing as far as Seth was concerned—now for more than one reason.

'Yeah, thanks.' Seth smiled, exceptionally glad he'd come here today. 'What's going on?'

But Dion was staring at him with a curious expression. 'What did you do to your jacket?'

Startled, Seth glanced down and saw streaks of something all over his lapels. He frowned, put his fingers to a spot and felt the slick dampness. Then he remembered—Green-Eyed Girl had grabbed his jacket as she'd snapped back at him. She'd held on to it tight. Now he knew why. She'd had some kind of slime on her hands and she'd wiped it all over him. The devious creature. He laughed, tickled and no less turned on. 'Oh, I don't know.'

He took it off—happy to—given he was still hotter than hot.

Dion still looked curious but Seth just jerked his head towards the team. 'What's going on?'

'Last couple of shots for the annual calendar shoot.'

'Really?' Seth grinned at the poor bastards. Most stood with their arms folded across their gleaming bare chests. His eyes narrowed. 'What have they put on you?' he asked the nearest one.

'Baby oil.'

A few started laughing again and smacking their chests like cavemen. 'Oh, she got us good.'

'I can still feel the sting of her palm,' one complained, rubbing his hand up by his shoulder. 'She's a sadist.' He rolled his eyes heavenward. 'But it was worth it.'

'Who got you good?' Seth tried to ask casually.

'Lena.'

Cue more smirks and body-slapping.

*Lena.* Oh, hell. Wasn't Lena the name of the woman Dion had told him about? The woman who had the power to save him from next week's nightmare so long as he could convince her to help him? The one he *needed*?

Hell, yes. Only, now he didn't want her to agree to his last-minute project plan, he wanted her to say yes to something else altogether. Seth gritted his teeth as a surge of testosterone rippled through his muscles—all masculine hunger and sexual curiosity. His curiosity was so rabid he was unable to resist asking exactly what they'd been up to with the luscious Lena. 'What did you do?'

'Asked her to rub the oil on,' one said with a shameless grin. 'Thought she'd refuse all haughtylike, but she didn't. She slapped it on all of us. And I mean *slapped.*'

The entire team erupted.

'Perfect!' the photographer shrieked, spinning, his finger holding down the shutter button as he caught them all. 'Keep talking.'

'You should have seen the look on her face.'

Oh, Seth had. 'Did she laugh?' He was still hearing that laugh; it had drawn him to her the way a magnet drew an iron filing. He'd been powerless to resist her pull.

'Nah, you never see that, she always holds it together. Cooler than a chilly bin.'

Uh, Seth didn't think so. He glanced down at the jacket in his hands, retrieved the few things he had in the pocket and dumped it in the rubbish. No getting oil stains out of that. He turned back, unable to resist asking more—to be sure it was her. 'She wouldn't be wearing a blue dress, would she? About this tall?' He gestured just above his shoulder. 'Dark hair, creamy skin, green eyes and curv—'

He broke off, recognising a little late that they'd all gone quiet and that he'd been about to get a little *too* detailed.…

'You noticed her,' said Ty, who Seth knew was the captain.

'I told you about her. Lena Kelly.' Dion pointedly looked from Seth to the rubbish bin and back again. 'PR and organisation and stuff.'

Yeah, definitely the one Dion had said Seth needed on board. She had the power to convince management to let him bring his boys here—the at-risk youth who needed not just a shot of discipline, but of inspiration, too. But Dion hadn't told him she was such a scorcher. And right now, wrong as it was, Seth had more of a fixation on that fact than he did on sorting the problem that had brought him here in the first place.

She definitely had a more valid reason than he did to be hanging out near the change rooms. What was more, she really *had* had her hands on all the boys. There was no smothering his chuckle.

The captain saw. 'Don't bother, mate, she's not interested.'

Oh. Seth cleared his throat. 'She's taken?' She'd better not be, or she shouldn't have been kissing him so hot—not just hungry, but famished. Aggression surged, hardening. He hated infidelity.

'No, but she refuses *everyone*. She almost flirts. You can see it in her eyes, but she never says what she's thinking,' Ty explained. 'Wish she would.'

'Got nice eyes,' one of the forwards grunted.

*Wicked* eyes.

Seth relaxed. He wasn't up for commitment and he wasn't going to be party to cheating. But he was more than happy to play.

'Got nice everything,' some other player piped up. 'But no one gets near. Totally untouchable.'

'Right.' Seth nodded, breathing deep to hide the outrageous victor's pleasure coursing through him. He had to stop himself puffing his chest out like some damn cockerel—because Not-Interested-Lena had been more than a little interested in him.

'You really do fancy her,' Dion stated quietly.

The entire team stopped laughing and stared at Seth. Suddenly they didn't look anywhere near as friendly—more like aggressive.

'Uh, no.' Testosterone resurged. He'd happily fight his corner, but he needed these guys onside if he was going to get them to help with the youth-aid project, so he went for deflection. 'Only noticing what you've all noticed.'

And now he noticed how the atmosphere had turned from teasing to protective. Which meant they respected her. Which meant she was no tease. Which meant he might have to be careful. He more than fancied her and badly wanted a fling. He'd had a dry spell for all of a month or so and she'd be a much-needed distraction from the construction consent issues he had coming out of his ears. And okay, he was totally hot for her. From the answering heat in her kiss, he knew he could get her to say yes. So long as her no-dating policy wasn't because she was holding out for a husband. Marriage wasn't in his deck of cards.

'She'll knock you back,' said Ty. 'She doesn't date anyone famous.'

But Seth wasn't famous in the way these guys were famous. Ten minutes ago she hadn't recognised him, nor had she knocked him back. In the right mood, Lena Kelly wasn't untouchable at all.

Dion's eyes had that delighted gleam that came on when he saw a building he wanted to acquire. 'I reckon you'd have more luck than most.' He turned to Ty. 'Want to make a bet?'

'No.' Seth instantly stamped on that. This conversation had gone more than far enough already. 'Never bet on a woman. Bad karma.'

Dion glanced, his laughter easy. 'Quite right. And we've pushed it enough with Lena today. Imagine what she'd do if she heard us now?'

The entire team cracked up again. The photographer practically bounced with excitement as he snapped off shots.

Dion looked smug. Seth suspected the bet comment had

been to provoke his reaction. Ruthless bastard. But Seth smirked, too—it took one to know one.

'So this is going to be the calendar, huh?' He knew his change of topic wasn't going to fool Dion. The captain was watching him as well but he tried anyway. 'You guys must just love this.'

'Oh, sure.'

Some of the guys groaned.

'Need you all back in the shot now,' the photographer called.

As they lined up his thoughts derailed. The temperature of that kiss had been surreal—like being submerged into a spa after a day on the snow, bringing out goose bumps even though you were burning. Your body couldn't decide if it was pleasurable or painful—just intense, hellish good. He was hurting for more of the supposedly untouchable Lena. The urge bit to the bone. He liked nothing more than a challenge and a chase. Used to success, he figured there was no reason why he couldn't get her to agree to *both* propositions. All he had to do now was find her.

'Coming through!'

Seth's body recognised the slightly husky edge to the singsong voice before his brain did. Predatory instincts rose, focus sharpened. He had to turn slightly to the side to force himself to relax. This was a challenge, yes, but not one for public consumption. The guys were cheesing it up for the camera, but he sensed their attention snap to him the second they heard her, too. They wanted to see what was going to happen. Which meant that, right now, *nothing* was going to happen. Later on? Absolutely everything.

He tried to act nonchalant, but it would be abnormal not to look, so as the heel tapping neared he glanced over. She was hidden by a wall of shirts—holding them up high and out front like a curtain—but he recognised the dress. His body acted as if it had met its dream mate and he gripped hard on his bunching muscles.

'Thanks, Lena,' said Dion. 'Hang them over there for us, will you? They'll need to shower after this. Don't want that oil over all the clothes.'

Seth knew Dion had just directed another speculative glance at the rubbish bin where his jacket was now in residence. But he wasn't going to say a word.

'Lena, this is Seth Walker,' Dion added. 'Seth, this is our ever efficient PR queen, Lena.'

Seth watched for a reaction as she heard his name. While he didn't expect everyone in the country to know his face, his name was more out there. But she was terribly busy hanging those shirts—still hiding. When she finally turned, her expression was schooled into one hell of a poker face. No wonder the team called her untouchable. He thought she should definitely play some kind of…poker.

He stared blankly for a second before shaking the stripping fantasy free and focusing harder. She wasn't looking up at him, so he couldn't see if that gleam was there. Her lipstick was fixed but there was that extra fullness of her mouth. Frustrated desire flooded him and he cursed the presence of an entire rugby squad.

Seth Walker. Of course that was who he was. Lena didn't need Wikipedia to know all about him. She should have recognised him earlier. She remembered his name from when he sold off some scheme for kazillions to a big corporate conglomerate and she should have recognised his face from the about-town sections of the paper and the women's mags. The guy was the most wanted accessory of every beautiful socialite in the city scene. In fact the guy *owned* half the central city—was responsible for all those warehouse conversions into cool apartments and hip restaurants and clubs. He was so driven in his career he made these athletes look like Tuesday-night social-sport amateurs. His projects would always come before his private life.

That lost him a lot of points.

The demerit gave her enough chill to be able to look his way and manage an impersonal, professional smile. But she couldn't quite meet his eyes and her heart hiccupped when she saw he wasn't wearing his jacket any more. He must have figured what she'd done to it and got rid of it. She glanced round the room, saw the tip of a sleeve poking out of the corner bin.

Right. She glanced quickly back at him, trying not to melt at the smile and the brilliant blues—and did he just shake his head a fraction?

Yes, from the non-reaction of the guys in the room she knew he hadn't said anything about what had happened in the corridor. They were unusually quiet right this second, but maybe the photographer had had a diva moment and told them all to behave, because she was certain Seth Walker hadn't done a brag.

That fact earned him several points back. The way his shirtsleeves clung to his broad shoulders scored him more than a few bonus ticks, as well.

Unasked, her brain continued digging out info. Bachelor of the Decade was the headline that screamed at her. Bachelor for Life if his behaviour ten minutes ago was anything to go by. Without doubt he played the field. Any man who got that close and kissed random women the second he had the chance ought to be given a wide berth.

*Ought to be.*

But Lena wasn't feeling as cautious as she should any more. No, she was giddily glad the sexy stranger wasn't a new starter for the team. He had nothing to do with rugby. He and Dion had to be mates and she guessed he was here to check out the stadium—even the most successful business types got excited over an access-all-areas pass to the place. Her own excitement ratcheted up another notch. Technically Dion wasn't her boss—he'd been asked to manage the stadium by the council, while she was employed by the rugby club. So as Seth was merely the friend of a business colleague there'd be no hint of 'at work' conflict. Her panic had been for nothing. And now the long-dormant hormones racing round her body filled her head with wonderfully wicked, over-the-top fantasies.

She tried to quell them with some common sense—the stuff she'd been at pains to develop in the last year or so. She'd been on ice for so long in the dating realm, a total playboy type probably wasn't the sort she ought to warm up with. Then again, her inner imp whispered, he knew how to have *fun.* There was a reason he was so popular with women and it wasn't his oversized bank balance. He knew how to kiss. It was obvious he knew how to do so much *more* than kiss.…

Lena still wasn't ready for a romantic relationship—too busy rebuilding her career and family's respect. But surely there was no reason why she shouldn't have a good time with someone who wanted only the same and no more?

She felt him watching her—felt that *focus.* The all-sensual, mesmerising, irresistible attentiveness. Couldn't he be exactly the *right* guy to break her drought with? No complications, no confusion—it could stay that simple. She burned at the thought, her body so badly wanted to know his. But it was just a fantasy—she had no hope of pulling it off.

'Seth, I'm going to be stuck here for a few more minutes,' Dion said. 'Lena will take you up to the offices and you can talk to her. Take the scenic route, Lena—he hasn't been through this part of the stadium.'

Lena nipped the inside of her lip. Maybe Seth *had* said something. But she showed Dion's guests round the stadium all the time. It was part of her job, not an extraordinary request. 'Of course,' she answered politely, desperately trying not to blush. She turned away from him and watched the team break up from the group-in-the-shower shot instead. 'Not long to go now, guys.'

'You better have the refreshments ready,' one of them called out.

'Isotonics only.' She sent the group an apologetic smile. 'They're already in the fridge. Doc's orders.' She turned towards the door and, under the cover of their groans, looked at him. 'Mr Walker?'

He followed, his voice low enough for the others not to hear. 'Oh, no, please, call me Seth.'

Just hearing him speak sent heat frizzling from skin right through to bone. Her heart raced light-years ahead of her body as she walked out to the corridor.

*That* corridor.

She set a quick pace, fighting for composure as she stared fixedly at the concrete floor. Oh, she had to pull herself together because this was just embarrassing—had she time-warped into a teen experiencing her first stirrings of sexual desire?

'As you can see we've just come through the players' area.' She started the tour spiel for safety's sake. She could talk on auto—and keep talking until she could escape to her office. 'Now we're heading up to the corporate entertainment area. The boxes run the length of the stand.'

She started to get into the swing of it, telling him the details of the stadium, the history of the construction, the naming rights of the stands. But she was so on edge she gabbled it all too quickly. So she had to move on to player stories. And then player stats. Anything so she could keep babbling nonstop all the way to the executive space.

She was increasingly conscious of his height and his pantherlike smooth movement at her side. He was watching her too closely, not taking in the behind-the-scenes view of the stadium and the boys' backgrounds at all. Her skin tingled, her nerves twanged.

'Lena, I'm not interested in these stats,' he interrupted with arrogant dismissiveness when they got to the top floor and her office was a safe step away.

She stopped midway through her recital of some lock's weight issues. Slowly—trying to remain calm and collected—she looked directly at him. 'Well, what did you want to know?'

'Your stats. Every last detail.'

He took advantage of her stunned immobility and moved a step closer.

'I'm not interested in men,' he said wickedly. 'But *you* clearly are, so how about you memorise my details, as well? I'm Seth. I sell buildings. I'm six feet two, Sagittarius, single, suffering no communicable diseases.' He paused, the sparks in his eyes kindled. 'Spellbound.'

And she was sweating. She, who'd been hit on by all those boys downstairs and never once blinked, was melting on the spot. Because this was different. This was...*him* and he took up all her vision.

'You going to reciprocate?' Merciless, he kept her attention his captive, waiting for her to answer.

She couldn't say a thing, even though she *really* wanted to. But she'd breathlessly lost the snappy answer-back ability she'd had in the corridor.

'Let me help you out,' he offered with wicked charity. 'You're Lena. You're slim, sporty, stylish. Single.' He paused, apparently waiting for her to deny it.

She didn't, so he continued ticking off points.

'Sexy. Spontaneous.' He paused again, considering. 'A sensual sorceress.'

Okay, *that* was over-egging it. 'While you're too smooth, too suave, too successful.'

He moved closer. 'You're also suggestive, sassy, sarcastic. What else?'

A scatterbrain who was trying her damnedest not to squirm. 'A little stunned.' Hopelessly honest.

'Me too,' he purred smoothly. 'But I also think we're both stirred.'

It was impossible not to smile. 'You don't think you're coming on too strong?'

'Too strong?' His volume lifted, so did his brows. 'Honey, I'm reining in hard. I think you know what I'd rather be doing right now. I think you'd rather that, too. I'm just trying to dispense with the preliminaries as fast as possible.'

She didn't just feel the heat in her face, belly and chest, but her fingertips, her knees, her *toes*—she was blushing *everywhere.* The man was outrageous—and what was more, he pulled the hitherto undiscovered outrageous thread running deep within her.

'You know you owe me a jacket.' He upped the intensity of his focus as if he knew damn well he had her already.

Her hormones sizzled into high gear and her tongue loosened completely. Her self-restraint unravelled with it. 'Well, you owe me an apology.'

'For kissing you?' His chin lifted defiantly. 'Never going to be sorry for that.'

Her innards flamed; fortunately her mouth kept working. 'No, for your insulting insinuations before that.'

'Oh, those,' he said flippantly. 'Sure, I'm sorry.'

Lena took in his devilish, gleaming blue eyes and his wolfish, *un*apologetic smile. So assured, so confident, so sexy. Intent rippled from him and sent a wild surge of insanity pulsing through her. It carried her so far away she didn't stop to think. 'No, that's not good enough,' she sassed back at him, tumbling beyond her boundaries. 'You can do it properly over dinner.'

Seth froze to replay her words in his head. Had she just said what he thought? 'Over dinner?'

'I prefer a home-cooked meal.'

Seth clamped his teeth to stop his jaw dropping. The rest of his body was still shut down. Well, *almost* his entire body. Satisfaction slammed into every cell—the 'untouchable' had just ordered him to take her to dinner. At home.

For a moment she looked as if she couldn't believe what she'd said, either, but she blinked and then held his gaze with unmistakable challenge in her pale green eyes. Her brows lifted—as if she was waiting for him to rise to it.

Hell, yes, he was rising. He struggled to get his slain brain to operate. It took at least three endless seconds before he got a useful phrase together. 'When can you get out of here?'

The rosy pink across her cheekbones deepened. 'You can pick me up from Exit Four at 6:00 p.m.'

'Exit Four,' he repeated blankly. Then it clicked—of the stadium, of course. 'Right.'

He was so close now they were nearly touching. Powerless to resist, he breathed in a good look at her body again. Her curves beneath the elegant dress beckoned, his hands itched to undo the buttons. He noticed the slight shake of her fingers before she curled them into fists and when he looked back to her face he saw how her eyes had widened.

It wasn't fear. He'd seen plenty of fear in his opponents. But in Lena he saw heat deepening, darkening her green irises. Primitive pleasure flooded as the tide of power turned towards him. He forgot why he was here. He forgot all about the boys and the disaster that had killed their programme for next week. All that mattered was tightening the knot on this tryst.

'Any other requests—are you vegetarian or anything?' he asked. Now he could feel her trembling all over, but she didn't try to step back. He liked that about her.

Her chin lifted, despite the hitch in her breathing, as well. 'I like...very fresh—' she snuck a breath '—food.'

A wave of tension hit Seth, so extreme he was unable to do anything; even forcing a swallow hurt.

The woman wanted fresh.

He stared. There wasn't a single freckle on her smooth skin, something totally rare in this sun-struck country. It made him think of succulent berries and rich cream and he wanted to taste every inch of what she might offer. He wanted her to offer it all.

Her light green eyes lanced through him—suggestive and serious and summoning. She'd snatched the lead. When she'd started chattering nonstop about the team and not looking him in the eye he'd thought he was going to have to hunt hard and he'd started to, but all of a sudden she'd turned the tables and caught him neat in a heartbeat. The chase was always a fun part of a fling but he was happy to skip it this time. She'd named the time and place and he'd be there.

All the same, he held her gaze deliberately too long—testing. The moment stretched until her mouth tightened and she swallowed. A half second later she was the one to break eye contact, lowering her lashes. Yeah, she wasn't as filled with chutzpah as she made out. And, given her trembling and what those boys had said before about her always saying 'no', he knew this wasn't her usual modus operandi, which made it even more intriguing. Yet, for whatever reason, she clearly wanted to feel in charge of their dealings. So he'd let her think she was—for now.

Anticipation thickened the silence. He watched the slight but rapid rise and fall of her chest, the pulse madly beating at the base of her neck, the deepening red of her flush. He could almost read the secret, wanton wishes being written in the air. He was so close to pushing her back onto that desk and finishing what they'd begun outside that damn change room.

'You'd better get to Dion's office.' All husky, she turned her head away from him. 'He'll wonder where you are.'

The irony of it was he was here to see her. Hoping he could convince her to go in to bat for his boys. Only, Seth wasn't about to ruin the prospect of a fascinating evening by bringing up business now. He couldn't seem to care enough about it this minute, which was *wrong* when so many others were relying on him. But the embodiment of temptation before him was irresistible. He reversed the order of his plan—Lena, then the project.

He stepped back to let her be the boss. Reminded himself that breathing was necessary to life. Assured himself that very soon he'd touch her again.

'6:00 p.m.,' he confirmed before any feminine doubts surfaced and she tried to cancel. He could see her wavering, not looking at him. Sure enough she shivered, her body battling to contain conflicting emotions. Desire versus uncertainty. But he wasn't going to let her withdraw. It was too late, the chemical reaction had begun and the explosion was inevitable.

He'd only taken a couple of steps out of sight of her doorway when he heard it. The laugh. The husky, nervous but naughty laugh. The desire to inhale that intoxicating mix almost overpowered him. It had drawn him to her in the corridor, had been echoing in his ears since. His fists clenched as he fought the impulse to turn back and tumble her to the floor. He was damn well going to have that laugh beneath him before nightfall.

# CHAPTER THREE

LENA staggered round her desk and curled into her chair. She wanted to hide, laugh, cry. All at once. Had she just done that? Had she brazenly come on to *the* Seth Walker—insisting he take her on a dinner date? At *home*? She laughed even more helplessly than she had before. Then it turned into panic. She glanced at her watch. It was just after 5:00 p.m., which meant that she had less than an hour before she was going to...*what* exactly?

She froze for the next ten minutes, struggling to believe she'd voiced her desire so bluntly. Struggling to believe she'd *felt* that desire to such an extreme. Then she heard them, the male voices, that low drawl, then laughter. She braced, her heart stopping for a seriously damaging twenty seconds.

They didn't come to see her. Didn't even glance in as they passed by her open door. She heard Dion calling out goodbye, heard the footsteps fade. So he'd gone, the guy she'd all but offered herself on a platter to—*fresh.* Was he really going to come back?

Time twisted, slowed, tormented. Her embarrassment multiplied. Why would the guy who could have any woman in the world want her? Things like this didn't happen to Lena. The rugby guys asked her out only because she was famous for saying no, not because they meant it. She must have imagined the intensity of that whole thing. Seth was a playboy. Lena, while not an innocent in a few too many ways, was utterly one in the world of the one-night rendez-vous.

Oh, hell. She could laugh it off, right? He probably wasn't going to show anyway. She held out her hand and checked to see if the all-over trembling she felt inside was visible. Totally was. As the seconds ticked she knew she couldn't follow through. She'd been on another planet to think she could. She might once have been labelled a minx who tried to destroy a marriage, but she was no femme fatale. She never did this. Never thought about hot, sweaty, super-naughty sex.

Well, hardly ever.

Her heart thundered, splitting her body in two with its contrary desires—one half wanted to run far and fast to a safe, isolated corner, while the other half couldn't get past that so-carnal kiss and wanted more, more, more.

Maybe what she'd said to him earlier hadn't been that far off the mark. Maybe being around all those nearly naked men had somehow turned her sexual thermostat on high. Maybe it hadn't been Seth heating her so devastatingly, it had been the situation.

That would be it.

Except she'd been around all those semi-naked rugby boys so many times before and had never had this kind of reaction to any of them. Somehow Seth Walker had slid right beneath her rigidly imposed barriers and flicked her switch on high. And it had been so long, she couldn't seem to turn herself back off. She drummed her fingers on her tidy desk and as the clock ticked on her bravado seeped out. She'd call him and cancel, except she didn't have his number.

Oh, hell, she didn't want to wait round for either a no-show or an awkward end to what had been a simple flirt for him and a lightning bolt for her. She grabbed her bag a good ten minutes before she'd told him to meet her and started down the empty corridor, a second away from sprinting.

'Lena.'

Her skin crisped as if she'd been plunged into boiling oil. She turned slowly and saw him leaning against Dion's doorjamb. 'What are you doing here?' she asked, girlishly breathless.

His smile broadened. 'Waiting for you?'

'I said Exit Four.' Her heart stuttered like a first-generation machine gun. The reaction began instantly—his proximity heating her so fast she tingled all over.

'Oh, that's right,' he drawled, eyes twinkling. 'I forgot.'

She didn't think so; he was far too intelligent to forget anything like that.

'Exit Four...' He glanced at the wall and the signs that were so helpfully posted there. 'That's down that corridor, isn't it?'

Lena didn't answer yes because, if she'd been going to Exit Four, she should have turned left five paces ago.

'Lucky we bumped into each other here, isn't it, otherwise you might have been waiting for ages at Exit Four and thought I'd stood you up. But I'd never do that.'

He spoke softly, but she felt the light bite he intended. He knew she'd been going to bottle it and be the one to stand *him* up.

She just looked at him, at a loss for everything because he was wreaking havoc on her system again. As had happened the second she'd first seen him, nerves, hormones, *needs* began to shriek.

'Shall we get going?' He jerked his head towards the stairs.

Her mouth was gummed, so she couldn't get the 'sorry

but no thanks' out and he'd already cupped her elbow and started walking them down the stairs. Her response surged higher. Incredible how the sound of his voice and the lightest grip on her brought on such giddy anticipation.

She was melting—into a mess. This wasn't going to work. She'd never spoken so suggestively in her life. In her last relationship it had been her ex who'd done the running; only at the end had she acted so desperately. Now she'd been more forward than she could believe, to someone so out of her league. Seth Walker was probably used to having women in his bed who did the splits five ways while swinging from a chandelier. She'd never been anything better than average in anything, not even sex. Her best course of action was a speedy withdrawal before she made more of an idiot of herself.

'I'm sorry about your jacket,' she muttered as they got to the entrance level.

'No, you're not.' He laughed. 'But that's okay, it wasn't a favourite.'

She walked with him across the car park, because she couldn't decide how to phrase her escape and because he moved with such assurance it was easier to go with him than against him. He'd put sunglasses on and she couldn't read his expression. She'd have put hers on, too, except she was holding her bag in a death grip and couldn't relax her fingers enough to operate the catch.

'This is mine.' He stopped by a beautiful gleaming black car. Its design spoke volumes—not some flashy low-to-the-ground sports number with a huge stereo system like most of the rugby guys drove, but sleek, solid, offering extreme comfort. 'You ready to go?' he asked.

'Actually, no.' She tried to smile back but her mouth was too stiff. 'This was such a… We don't have to do dinner. I don't know what came over me,' she mumbled. 'I was just being…being…'

'Provocative?'

Yes, she had been. Only, now she'd provoked his reaction, she didn't think she could handle it.

'Stupid,' she corrected, staring at the car rather than him. 'Look, I'll catch the bus. I'm sorry you had to come back here.'

'You're not catching the bus.' He smiled, totally friendly and not at all wolfish. Well, she didn't think so—she couldn't see his eyes. 'At least let me drop you home.'

Oh. Lena breathed. He'd capitulated easily—she'd been reading this wrong. He wasn't that interested. And she refused to admit to that sudden disappointment. 'No, I'm okay. I'll get the bus.'

'I'm here anyway, I'm driving back through town…' He still looked friendly, but like he didn't really mind either way. 'Be silly to waste the gas.'

As she hesitated he flicked a button and unlocked the car. She shouldn't refuse. She'd look silly and rude and hadn't she been silly and rude enough to him? She didn't want to look any more pathetic than she already did. 'Okay, but I'm really sorry for wasting your time.'

She was even more sorry she didn't have the guts she'd had an hour before. She slid into the car, felt the leather practically embrace her. He pulled out of the park instantly, the engine so smooth it was almost inaudible.

'I'm disappointed,' he said. 'I was looking forward to cooking up something fresh for you.'

Despite the gentle airconditioning, Lena's temperature surged and butterfly wings beat in her belly. But he'd spoken so blandly there wasn't any undertone going on, right? 'You caught me at a bad moment when I was…wasn't thinking.'

'Now I'm even more disappointed.' His lips curved. 'I

thought I'd finally found a woman who'd hold her own with me. I was excited about that.'

Hold her own? Okay, the undertone *was* there and searing images filled her head—ones where pleasure was extreme and mutually exhausting. 'I think we should forget about what happened this afternoon,' she mumbled.

'No, you don't.' He suddenly laughed. 'And I *can't.* Anyway, I need to offer you a genuine apology and you do owe me for the jacket.'

Did he have to laugh? It was too seductive. 'You can send me the bill and you don't need to apologise, your assumption wasn't that bad. Or surprising, considering how it must have looked.'

His grin widened, which wasn't right, because she wasn't trying to tease him, she was trying to engineer an almost dignified exit.

'I apologise anyway,' he said. 'And as for your account, I'd prefer your time over your money.'

A smooth line. A turn of his head that spelt intimacy. Her hot-for-him hormones soared—turning her back into that malleable toy with 'his to play with' on the label. She took a quick breath and told herself to calm down. It was mad to feel his every word and glance so intensely.

He drove confidently, sliding along the thinnest of lanes with nerve-twanging speed, asking briefly for directions. She gave them as best she could, given her whirling thoughts and seesawing intentions.

'How long have you worked at the stadium?' he asked.

Easy conversation. Thank goodness. 'Nearly eighteen months.'

'And you don't mind being the only woman among all that testosterone?'

'There are women working there—in catering, front of house.'

'But not with you.'

'No.' Admittedly she'd liked it that way at the start. She'd found that women judged more than men, their approval was harder to win and easier to lose and she'd been wary about making new friends. She'd steered well clear of the wives-and-girlfriends club and even further from the behind-the-wife's-back mistresses. But now she was happier than she'd ever been and she'd love to find some girls to hang with. Trouble was now she was so busy at work she didn't have much time.

'So the guys don't bother you?' he asked, the tease apparent in his tone. 'I imagine they can be pretty demanding at times.'

'You mean like the baby oil request?' She giggled. 'I don't mind them, they're just goofing. My brother was a national basketball rep, my father the assistant coach.' She shook her head. 'I've been surrounded by packs of competitive, sporting males my whole life, I know how to handle jocks and jerks.'

'Yeah, you left your mark on a couple today, that's for sure.' He laughed, too. 'So does your brother still play?'

'He's in the States now on a full scholarship at one of those Ivy League places.'

'Impressive.'

'Yeah, he's pretty amazing.' Her kid brother wasn't just a stellar athlete, but a genius academic, as well. But even he couldn't hold a candle to their super-gifted sister. Lena loved them both, was proud of them both. And wanted them to be even just a little proud of her. So she was working on it. 'My place is next on the left.'

He turned the car into her driveway and she braced herself to begin the goodbye she'd been mentally practising. 'Thanks for—'

'You know, I was hoping you'd change your mind,' he

interrupted. Taking off his sunglasses, he swivelled to face her. He knew what he was doing. Anyone who looked into those blue eyes would be hypnotised into saying 'absolutely' to everything.

'Invite me in,' he said bluntly. 'I'll cook. Won't take an hour and your debt's paid.' A so-easy deal from a wicked expression.

She didn't answer. At that moment, she simply couldn't.

'It's too nice a night to dine alone.' He was shameless about using that gorgeous smile.

Seth Walker was a winner and she knew why. She also knew that if she let him in now, there was a very high chance he wouldn't be leaving again 'til the next morning.

He knew that, too.

*That* was the decision.

He waited, holding her hostage with just that look. She couldn't drag her gaze away. It hovered between them— knowledge, awareness, honesty. With his sunglasses off, she saw the hunger in him. Her hormones rejoiced and the sensible, safe, walk-away decision of twenty minutes ago got fried in the heat roiling inside her. This might be a first for her but that didn't make it bad. Crazy confidence flared, coiled inextricably around recklessness. In that instant she knew she'd do whatever the hell she wanted.

*He* was what she wanted. She *would* be the vixen she'd once been branded. Just for one night.

She undid her seat belt. 'Okay, you can cook dinner. But I'll help.'

She turned from his victory smile and got out of the car to unlock her flat. She was halfway across her lounge when she heard her front door shut with a thud.

She paused; her sense of intimacy screamed higher. So did her pulse. So did her until-this-afternoon-dead sex drive. Blood rushed and hunger pooled, relentless in its demand.

She turned to look at him. Yes. This wasn't a desire to fill an emotional need—a renowned playboy wasn't the guy for that. But she was sure he could satisfy the physical void she was suddenly acutely aware of. He was the most impressive man she'd ever met. And given where she worked, that was saying something. It seemed she'd been stabbed with an adrenaline injection. Okay, a lust injection.

'Nice place.' He carelessly dropped his keys onto a table near the door.

'You sound surprised.' She watched him slowly turn full circle in the centre of her room. The opportunity to ogle him was too tempting. Just looking made her more restless. A tall man in suit trousers and a cotton shirt—how could so simple be so sexy?

Erotic urges clamoured for her to act. In part because she couldn't believe this actually might happen. It was as if she was driven to push it fast now, for fear he'd change his mind—that this was all a joke or something. But she could hardly jump his bones two seconds after letting him into her house. She tensed her pelvic muscles to get the hot, hungry feeling under control, only that made it worse.

It was sick. And, frankly, sensational.

'No flatmates?'

'Not right now,' she squawked an answer. She'd been thinking about getting a flatmate to help expand her woefully small social life but hadn't had the time to advertise yet.

'It's very comfortable.' His attention lingered on her big sofa. It faced a big TV screen. Yes, she had a sub to the satellite sports channel.

Dazed by the rushing feeling, she half managed to keep the conversation going. 'You didn't expect that?'

'For some reason I thought you'd have a more minimalist approach.'

Lena laughed. This was no cool, clutter-free room; instead almost every area could be sprawled on. The oversized sofa and big armchair were covered with rich fabrics, rafts of cushions and a couple of soft wool throws tossed over for good measure. Which was the point. She wanted her home to offer comfort, not be filled with the trophies of siblings, or photos of other people's success. The house where she'd grown up had been filled with mementos of family glory—none of which had been hers. It had been the environment where success and achievement were all that mattered. Here there were no tick charts or training programmes or study guides pinned to the walls. This place was her sanctuary.

'I just wanted a place to relax, you know?' She tried to joke but sounded too husky.

He faced her directly, his blue eyes bright. 'If I get onto that sofa, I don't think I'll get off it again.'

'Then no sofa just yet.' She flicked her tongue over her hot, tight lips. 'I'm hungry.'

'Hungry is good,' he said softly. 'Because I've got lots to offer.'

O-o-okay. So the entendres were appalling. And irresistible.

'But, you know, I didn't get to the shops.' He shrugged apologetically. 'Didn't get anything fresh.'

'You were waiting at the stadium the whole time?' She had only just worked it out now. It had been Dion she'd heard leave.

He looked softly amused. 'Well, I didn't want you to change your mind and disappear on me.'

She felt the now familiar heat burn hotter in her cheeks. Yes, he'd known she'd been going to. She turned towards the kitchen. 'I'm afraid I don't have much in my pantry.'

'Why don't you let me be the judge of that?' He brushed

past unnecessarily close, the slight touch sizzling that tiny patch of skin.

Oh, hell, were they still talking with double meanings?

Smiling at her insane need and even more insane thoughts, she counted to three before following him to the kitchen. She perched on one of the stools by the bench and tried not to stare.

Clearly he'd noted the nothing much in the fridge because he was now frowning into the small freezer, obviously not a fan of the microwave meals she usually existed on. She nipped her lower lip, stopping herself from justifying their tragic existence, but she often worked late and was tired when she got in.... Yeah, so much for *fresh*.

'You like pizza?' He slammed the freezer door and spun to face her. 'I know a great place that does delivery.'

'Your world-famous crusts?' She knew it was the pizza business he'd launched then sold when still in his teens that had netted him his first million.

'And buns.' He chuckled. 'You've tried them before?'

She shook her head. 'I don't usually do fast food or take-away.'

His grin widened. 'Didn't think so.' Still that damn doubletalk. 'Means we'll have half an hour or so to wait for it,' he noted with a teasing lilt. 'What do you think we should do?'

His gaze met hers and held it firm. Time expanded.... It might have been an hour or so before she answered.

'Have a drink,' she croaked eventually. 'Chat.'

They had to talk. Even just for ten minutes. That meant they'd have talked for about fifteen minutes before fling-ing into bed together. 'So—' she fought for some kind of conversation starter '—you're not even Italian and you sold everyone pizza.'

'Pizza's a universal thing.' He reopened her fridge and

pulled a bottle of wine from the depths with a pleased smile. 'I wanted to see if I could take an already established product and compete against the big corporates in a new way.'

'But then you sold out to them.' She set two glasses on the bench between them.

He chuckled as he poured, seeming to appreciate her challenge to his entrepreneur credibility. 'I'd proved my point and was ready to move on.'

'Oh, right.' She lifted her glass and jabbed a little more for the fun of it. 'You don't just get them to a level of success so you can then sell, make the money and bail before they crash and burn?'

His gaze went rapier sharp. 'No. If they crash and burn that's because the management that took over was incompetent.'

She smiled wickedly. 'So it's not that you're dealing in smoke and mirrors? Making something look amazing when really there's very little there. Nothing that has durability.'

'Well, the tee shirts are still going. The pizza, they took the marketing concepts and made them their own. The buildings are increasing their value—what's the basis for all this doubt?'

'The fact that you always move on,' she said simply. The guy never stuck at anything for more than a few years, frequently less, which was why the property game suited him—acquire, improve, sell. 'Isn't it that you don't actually believe in your own products?'

'No, it's because I have a low boredom threshold.' His eyes glinted with naughty undercurrents. 'Once something's up and running, I'm no longer interested. It's the challenge of getting it together and out there that I like. And I like to keep my independence.'

She gripped her glass tighter. 'So you're not interested in

the challenge of continuing growth or developing depth in any of your projects?'

'No.' That glint flashed even brighter. 'That's not really my thing.'

There was the subtext. He loved the initial challenge, but was so a no to seeing it grow to something bigger. Just like his relationships with women? Well, that was fine. She already knew there could only be this, right now....

She didn't want a relationship. She was doing well—loving her job, loving her freedom out of the family shadow. She didn't want any slide backwards into neediness and she feared that if she let a guy in for too long, she'd lose her hard-earned independence and confidence. But one night wouldn't be too long.

She realised he was watching her with that intense focus again.

'So what about you?' His glint became an all-out blaze. 'Let's get to that killer sofa and you can tell me more about how you handle those rugby stars.'

She led the way back to the lounge. 'There's not that much to tell. I'm only the PR administrator.'

'Slash team organiser slash wardrobe mistress slash stadium Girl Friday.'

'You got me on a good day.' She shrugged it off with a smile. 'Most of the time it's the usual running around chasing people and paperwork.' She stopped to put her empty glass on the low table in front of the sofa and turned.

He was right behind her. With the quickest movement she'd ever seen he ditched his glass on the table and took the last half step to be within breath-mingling distance.

She swallowed. 'This probably isn't a good idea.'

'No, it's a fantastic idea,' he assured her.

She moistened her lips. But it didn't cool them—nothing could stop the temptation bubbling over. Purely sexual.

Blatantly provocative. Honestly, if she didn't have an orgasm soon she was going to go insane. She was halfway there now. Who knew that nymphomania was actually some flu-like virus you could be struck down with in a matter of minutes? Well, now Lena did, because all she could think about was sex—him and her and heat. Touching and skin and tongues and other body parts merging and teasing and satisfying.

'This can only be the one night,' she blurted.

It had to stay hers to control. It wasn't about letting him do what he wanted. It was what *she* wanted—good age-old fun with an expert. She wanted the fantasy. She'd been so damn good for so damn long. Just a few hours for herself couldn't hurt, could it? Not with Mr Single. Mr Playful. Mr Perfect-for-One-Night.

He was smiling that irresistible smile and she was so mesmerised she didn't move as he lifted a hand and traced her jaw, then her mouth, with his index finger. His eyes tracked his action, intently focused and *promising*. 'Whatever you want.'

His simple charm reinforced her belief that this could be light and easy. His simple touch made it impossible for her to deny herself the incredible pleasure of more.

She met his hot, good-humoured gaze and her long-hidden playfulness broke free. 'That's right.'

# CHAPTER FOUR

SHE'D never known her blood could simmer.

'Something else, isn't it?' Seth murmured with a gentle shake of his head. 'The chemistry.'

Lena stood with her legs locked so she stayed upright. It was more than anticipation, it was need—several layers deep. She blanked the raw ache buried in her heart. This was *physical* fulfilment.

'You're beautiful,' he muttered, tracing her lips again.

She mirrored his action, putting her finger on his lips. 'No lines.' It wasn't necessary. This could just be what it was. She didn't want false words.

His eyes narrowed but his smile widened. 'Not lines. Absolute truth. I wanted you the second I saw you laughing in the corridor.'

Pleasure skidded into her. Okay, she'd let him feed her just that line. It was a good one.

She watched him draw nearer. This wasn't going to be an impulsive, unexpected kiss. This time it was going to be premeditated and foreseeable and all of a sudden nerves ate up her anticipation. In the split of a second, she didn't think she could do it. She swallowed, her brain suddenly crammed with thoughts and doubts and confusion. Was this crazy? Could this really be as easy as it seemed?

'Lena?' He froze as he registered her tension. Then she

saw something like horror on his face. 'You have done this before, right?'

Sex? Yes. So quickly? No.

She gave a slight nod. 'But I might have forgotten how,' she mumbled, her blush nothing but embarrassment now.

He took a couple of breaths, his grin rueful. 'You know, we don't have to go for gold if you don't want to. We can just play for a while and if you say the word, I'll stop.'

She didn't want him to stop but she really appreciated his gentlemanly attitude. 'No, I want to have a…good time,' she breathed, trying to be blunt but opting for a euphemism in the end. 'I've been frisky since we kissed and I'm so close but so damn far. But I want to. Really, really want to.'

His breath was sharp drawn then. She felt him release it in a laugh hot across her forehead.

'Shouldn't be a problem,' he muttered, lips skimming her skin. 'What do you want me to do?'

'Everything,' she answered, drinking in his masculinity, tired of repressing her feminine desire for it. From the moment she'd opened her eyes this afternoon and seen him gazing right through her, she'd been aching for him to take her apart.

He gazed down her body and she saw his expression transform from hotly amused to predatory. That was the look she needed—the one where basic drive couldn't be fully hidden beneath suave charm. She wanted the animal in him, because he totally aroused the animal in her. And if it was all animal, there could be no thought.

Her breathing quickened. Her blood quickened.

He smiled, slowly. Then he bent his head and touched his lips to hers. For a second or two he kept it light and gentle, then he seemed to give in to the urge and crushed her. Temptation was riding him as hard as it was her. Thank goodness.

He slid his arms around her, pulling her close against him, controlling where her body touched his. She let him because where he held her was where she wanted to be and she wanted to feel his strength. So she clung, melding, unable to believe the heat. She kissed him back as she had in the corridor. Hot and hungry and offering so much more than her mouth. The wave of delight rose swiftly and she badly wanted to get to the end—to have everything from him this instant. Except it couldn't possibly be over in five seconds and if he kept kissing her like that it was going to be. She broke free and took a step back.

He looked pained. 'You're saying the word already?'

'Oh, no,' she gasped. 'I'm just…breathing.' She wanted it both fast *and* slow. Total fulfilment. She wanted the entire cake and to eat it all herself. She gazed at him, honestly couldn't believe he was this hot and that for tonight he was all hers. 'I don't want to lose it too quickly.'

'Too quickly? That's usually something the guy has to worry about.' He chuckled and took hold of her hand. 'I thought you wanted to come?'

'I do…but…' Oh, this was so overwhelming.

Laughing, he pulled her back into his arms but cradled more than controlled. She could feel the vibrations of his humour.

'Tell you what…' His sentence drifted and she felt him laugh again, heard it in his voice when he whispered in her ear, 'Half an hour before I go below your waistline.'

She jerked—putting her palms on his chest and leaning away to look in his face. *Half an hour?* No, no, no.

'Oh, it *has* to be half an hour now,' he teased. 'The look on your face.'

'What do you mean, half an hour?' Instinctively she spread her fingers wider, enjoying the solid feel and the slam of his heart against her palm. 'What are you going to do? Set your timer or something? You think this is paint by numbers?'

'It'll slow us down—' he leaned close again, breathing close to her skin '—just enough to send you insane.'

'I already am.' Shivers of wickedness trammelled down her spine. Pure delight at his playfulness…but half an hour did seem like twenty-nine minutes too long.

He tilted her face up and looked devilishly into her eyes. 'This is about what you wanted, right? And if you want to have a good time, you have to leave yourself in my hands.'

His hands were good. They went lower, stroking down her back, chasing the shivers and electrifying her skin. Skilful fingers stroked round her waist, sliding upwards to smooth over her breasts and brush against her nipples.

She nearly came then and there, her nerves so tight she compressed her muscles hard to try to control the escalating drive.

'Oh,' she moaned. Who really was in charge here? And what did it matter? 'You know, fast will be fine,' she breathed. 'I don't know what I was thinking.' She framed his face with her hands, laughing more than a little desperately. 'Just ignore everything I said and let's get on with it.'

She rocked against him, unable to stop need driving her now. There was nothing, *nothing,* but fire between them.

'Never.' The predatory look sharpened to pure masculine pleasure. 'Half an hour, Lena. Let's see how you cope.'

The smile she saw just before he kissed her told her she was in glorious trouble. Sure enough, less than thirty seconds later she wasn't coping at all well. His hands stroked and teased—caressing light and then firm. He kissed sweet, then dirty. Every second he pulled her closer and closer still, his hands tickling the back of her neck, tracing down her spine, sliding round her waist to move up to the curve of her breasts. Wildly she moved against him, desperate to feel his touch all over—especially inside. Surely it was half an hour now? It felt as if it had been for ever.

Through dazed eyes she saw his were sharply focused, burning and determined. His fingers flicked, undoing the first few buttons on her dress, pushing aside the silky fabric. He bent her back, holding her weight easily with one arm while he kissed his way across and seared her skin. She clung to his waist, barely able to stay standing.

His hands wandered into the open dress, cupping her breasts. He kissed her neck, her collarbone and lower, stealing across her curves; through the lace bra she felt his tongue, the hunger of his hot, wet mouth. Her eyes closed as he muttered his appreciation, and told her what he wanted to do in about twenty minutes or so. He relished her as much as she did him and she liked it. Her breathing deepened as her skin tingled. Her nipples were suddenly so sensitive and with every stroke of his tongue across them they sent teasing rhythmic surges to her womb. Those deep, secret muscles clamped in response, winding higher, hotter. Her fingers curled into his shirt as the sensation sharpened. Her whole body contracted beneath his simple, relentless attention.

'Oh, no.' She was so taut she couldn't even scream; it was a squeak.

'Just let it happen,' he murmured, easily supporting her when in the instant of ecstasy her strength failed.

She'd never had an orgasm this way, this easily, this sweet and savage. She panted, quickly trying to recover some kind of control, but she soon discovered that that hit of pleasure was merely a precursor. Now her body was frantic for more. She was desperate to be naked. Desperate to be possessed. She ground her pelvis hard against his, wanting to force an end to the void there.

She was so damn hungry to have him, to touch him. Her

eyes shot open. Of course. There was nothing to stop her touching *him* now. A resurgence of energy poured through her and excitement flared. She spread her hands wide on his arms, then dropped to his waist, slipping underneath the shirt to discover the definition of his body. Eye-poppingly sharp definition.

'What are you doing?' he growled.

She smiled slowly, enjoying the power surge as she read the heat in his expression. 'It's only half an hour before *you* get below the waistline. *I* can access any area any time I want.' And she was quite happy to torment him, given that was exactly what he was doing to her.

She chuckled as she moved, her hands zeroing in on the target. He might be happy to skirt around the danger zone, but she was going straight for the kill, unfastening his trousers. He didn't stop her but his molten eyes sizzled. She drowned in his huge dark pupils, seeing herself in them—her desire reflected.

She pushed forward, taking her weight again. 'What's the matter?' she asked softly. 'You're not sure you can cope?'

She lifted his shirt, he raised his arms and she stripped it from him, totally focused on every inch of skin as it was revealed. She felt liberated, thinking about nothing but the body before her.

'You like?' He sounded rusty.

'Yeah, I told you earlier,' she answered. 'It's not only men who like to look.' She ran a feather-light fingertip across his shoulders, felt the faintest quiver beneath her touch. 'You have an amazing body.'

He really did. Incredibly fit—he clearly worked out a lot. His muscles were even more sharply defined than the rugby boys', which meant he had to put some serious hours into the gym. 'You've got what I want.' His body was everything she wanted. Maintaining eye contact, she moved her hand south into total danger territory. She gulped. 'Maybe *more* than what I want.'

His muscles bunched; she could feel him holding his breath, too.

'You might want to be careful,' he muttered.

She sent him a coy look from beneath her lashes, while her hand stroked—anything *but* coy. Inside she smiled giddily. 'You said half an hour.'

He grinned despite his gritted teeth. He even managed to talk through them. 'Yeah, and then you're going to be in such trouble.'

She leaned forward. 'Oh, I know that now.' She pressed her open mouth on his hot neck.

His hands grasped her shoulders so hard she was forced to look back up at him. As soon as she did he swooped. His tongue invaded her mouth in a way that left her in no doubt as to what that other magnificent part of him was going to do the second his inner timer went off. She went boneless against him, welcoming his plundering assault. She couldn't wait. Her hands swept up and down his hot torso, pausing to push the trousers and boxers from his hips so she could feel his tight butt. She moaned, pulling him against her.

She let go of every inhibition, every doubt, every thought or care in the world and just *felt*. She took total pleasure in touching him and in his touch. Absolute freedom from emotional complications—from expectations—there were none.

'Ding, ding, ding.' He moved fast, stealing the next beat of her heart and the initiative. She was on the floor before she could gasp, while he was above her already. He was kneeling, with his hands on either side of her, and his eyes met hers, flashing the naughtiest smile she'd ever seen.

He lifted one hand and toyed with the hem of her dress. 'Time's up.'

She pressed her knees hard together—to stop herself from splaying her legs wide. But he knew because the wickedness in his expression sent the mercury soaring. And it seemed he liked a game as much as she.

'You really think you can hold out?' he asked slyly.

'No.' She parted her legs. This was too good to waste more time waiting for.

'Mine to do with as I please.' He chuckled—satisfied—and undid the rest of the buttons with teasing, cavalier fingers.

'No,' she argued huskily, writhing under his gentle caresses. 'You're mine to please me.'

He inclined his head. 'Same thing.' He spread her dress, bent and kissed her, his hands working first to remove her bra and then skimming up her thighs to her knickers. Slowly, too damn slowly, he tugged them down.

Seth watched her expression as he bared her body. Her eyes were luminous—pale green glittering in the thinnest of rings around huge black pupils. Her lips cherry red from desire, not lipstick. Satisfaction jolted at how urgent her need was. She intended to ravish him. His erection strained harder. He didn't think he'd ever met a woman so hungry. Deeply, beautifully hungry for pleasure. From him.

Her gaze devoured his body. Her hands stroked, she propped up on her elbows and licked his nipple, her tongue lashing stronger than he expected. The response in his blood was stronger than he expected, too. He burned, unsure he could stand the pressure of this, the hottest moment of his life. He pushed her back and she moaned when he ran his tongue from her navel to her breast. Yeah, it was his turn to taste.

Seth was used to women trying to impress him. He knew it was because of his bank balance more than anything, but women fluttered their lashes and pulled their best moves.

And he appreciated it, he did. But the woman writhing beneath him now was in no way trying to impress. She was almost out of it with pleasure, her eyes blind with passion.

'Lena,' he murmured, licking her from breast to breast with slow, teasing strokes, swirling around each taut peak. He liked that it was *him* rousing her this high, this intensely.

'Mmm.' She was lost in sensation, unbelievably warm and responsive. Her hips rose, rotating—no longer merely inviting, but demanding. And he was powerless to deny that demand. He couldn't deny *himself.* The need to taste her, to satisfy her, overwhelmed him. Yeah, ecstasy was all she wanted—and that was what he wanted, too, right? Nothing could give him greater pleasure this second.

He grinned as he kissed down her torso. Her breathless cries increased—pace, volume, pitch as he neared her most sensitive part. He thanked the stars her desire had conquered her defences and she'd given in to the electricity between them.

His focus sharpened as he spread her wide and tongued her soft and then deep. Her thighs shook, her fingers clenched, her screams hoarse. Yeah, he wanted this and more. He gripped her harder. Her uninhibited response was stunning and made him push her beyond it. He kissed deeper, stroked, teased, twisted—everything and anything to make her convulse with ecstasy again and again.

When he finally rose to all fours, her eyes were closed but she had that smile on her face. He waited expectantly. Saw her shoulders lift just a little, and then it emerged. A couple of chuckles. Low and breathy but powerful enough to drive him crazy.

'You're incredible,' he said, sliding his hand up her thigh with a strong, foreign feeling of possessiveness. He wanted to know more. She was an unpredictable enigma. He wanted to unwrap her—wanted to know why she was so hungry, why she'd hesitated, why she'd done this with him and none of the others. Why she was famed for saying no when she clearly loved to say yes.

But first he wanted the rest of it.

Lena wriggled, restless for him to finally get that perfect piece of masculinity right into where she was wet and wanting and waiting. She'd had her orgasm—more than one—but it seemed they weren't enough. The ache inside could only be filled by finishing this off completely. And she wanted to see *him* finish.

She reached to hold his face between her palms, brought him down to kiss him. Her body rocked beneath his, begging for him to join with her. Passion overtook her initial tease. Suddenly wild again with need, she grabbed his tight butt and pulled him towards her, rubbing the head of his erection between her legs, and thrust her hips. 'Condom!' She screamed her demand before she lost her mind completely.

Panting, he flung back onto his knees, fingers digging through the mess of material for his pocket and his wallet. Working fast to roll on the protection.

Impatiently she watched the play of muscles under his gleaming skin as he moved, drinking in the rush of his breath and the pent-up energy in his actions. She moved restlessly. She couldn't wait any longer. He glanced up and caught her—his eyes dark, fierce, more potent than any drug. Swiftly he arched, covering her body with his. Held fast by his intent gaze, she stilled for that magical moment before it all changed.

It blazed in his face a split second before he moved. Pleasure, such pure, profound pleasure.

She gasped, sucking in a deep breath that she held for ever as the incredible feeling of him rippled through her. She shook her head, shivering from the inside out, her body convulsing with excitement. Through her fast-tunnelling vision she saw his hand clenching hard into a fist beside her. His knuckles marble white. She looked back up to his face and read the agony there, the painful determination to hold his control. Pure, power-filled delight bubbled from within, finding release in a breathy laugh. His tension broke and he smiled down at her. She bit her lip as the intensity within her sharpened to overwhelming and emotional. Her eyelids lowered—just enough for some respite from this attraction. He was so gorgeous and so focused on her and making her feel so good, it almost made her cry.

'Don't stop.' His fingers teased her lightly under her jaw. 'I like hearing you laugh.'

Oh, yes, he was nice. He moved and her split second of emotional hunger slipped as carnal delight resurged. She smiled but her laugh didn't sound, because just as it began he swooped to kiss her, breathing in her joy.

That kiss trebled her pleasure, and her eyes did water then as an intense feeling of happiness swamped her. She closed her eyes but opened deeper for him, arching, help-lessly inviting him to share with her in a way she'd never shared with another. Purely physical, yes, but purely free.

He wrapped his arms around her, his hands firmly draw-ing her closer until they were locked in a snug embrace, skin to skin, pressed together from lips to toes. She clung, her arms crossed tight across his shoulders as he moved powerfully into her. But also, just holding *him.* Close and caring. She felt more caring, and more cared *for* than she'd ever expected she would from a brief encounter. Despite the driving passion, the blatantly basic attraction that had pulled them to this point so fast and so ferociously, he was tender. And so good. As he moved within her, watching her, ensuring she got the pleasure she sought, her feelings deep-ened—she softened, welcomed, *gave.* Some secret part of herself slipped free, and in response he drew her ever closer, ever deeper, ever higher. His endurance overwhelmed her. Her hands slipped over the muscles working beneath the sweat-slicked skin of his back as he adjusted their position, increasing the pleasure of the friction between them, playfully rolling his hips.

Oh, the tease. The wonderfully wicked tease. So she teased back, drawing on feminine instinct. Trying a movement, a rhythm, a touch, a kiss—anything to tilt his control of their coupling. And it worked; she heard his gasp, felt his quiver and the resurgence of his muscles—his determination.

She smiled. She laughed. He growled.

And together they soared.

Her mind blanked, words meant nothing as touch spoke instead. The moment stretched with just the two of them in its rainbow bubble. She might have sighed, maybe screamed, she didn't know. Didn't care. All that mattered was the tumbling sensation, falling faster and faster until her consciousness was buried and all that remained was that emotion—happiness and completion and burning, blinding ecstasy.

## CHAPTER FIVE

THE morning sun stabbed Lena's eyelids, demanding she open them. But there was no way she'd ever move again. Every muscle ached. Most especially her heart. Yes, now reality intruded. The doubts so easily silenced last night screamed now. And there was that soft part of her already whispering, wishing—because he'd been wonderful, so playful and passionate and tender.

She frowned, refusing to be weak. She was in control here and this was just the one night. She couldn't let herself think she cared for him just because he'd been nice to her in bed. She couldn't let herself think this could become anything more. To ensure that, she knew there couldn't be any further interaction between them. The knots in her tummy tightened as she shifted to test her body. She breathed in sharply, knowing she was going to have to force some greater effort shortly. While it had been the most amazing night of her life, there'd be no replay. He was gorgeous and generous. He was also a very successful, rich player—definitely not someone she should hang with for long. Dynamite didn't do duration. It went *boom,* then was over.

'You even chuckle in your sleep, do you know that?'

Her muscles ignored her stern thoughts and warmed at his low tease. 'Do I?' She frowned, trying to stop the melt. 'Must have been a good dream.'

'That's what I figured.'

Just a dream—this had to be treated as lightly and as gently as that. A bubble that would float on a gentle breeze, out of the window, beyond sight. She didn't want to burst it, so she'd have to tread carefully—but firmly all the same.

She twisted to face him. Her stomach knots headed north, causing an ache in the centre of her chest. Saying no was going to be hard enough already, but now she could see the sleepy-cum-saucy expression in his eyes. With his overnight stubble and his hair tousled—by her passionate hands—he was the epitome of the irresistible lover.

She forced herself to sit up, 'I have to get going.'

'It's early.' Deeper, sleep-rusted, his words made her bones quiver.

She steeled her muscles and slipped out of the bed, quickly covering herself with her robe despite the fleeting stiffness the movement caused. 'I've got a lot to do. It's a busy time for the team. There's no such thing as an off-season.'

He rolled over, propped his head on his hand and managed to look even more the picture of morning-after wicked. 'So no lazy lie-in and I'm guessing you don't want to go to a café for breakfast or anything before work?'

'That's a nice idea,' she said crisply, turning away from him so she stayed on track. 'But it can't happen, sorry.'

'Can't happen today, or any other day?'

She froze, halfway across the floor to the door. He wasn't slow, was he? She inhaled and turned to face him. 'Any other day. Sorry.'

He still lay reclined like a glorious bronze sculpture. 'So that's it? You're giving me the boot? Going to make me do the walk of shame home?'

She wrinkled her nose. 'Not the walk of shame.'

'No?' he drawled. 'You're not having some regrets right now?'

She blinked and then forced a smile, faking confidence in both her decision and her ability to enforce it. 'Oh, no, I don't regret what happened at all. It was amazing. But…'

'But it was just the one night.'

'That's what we agreed,' she reminded him carefully.

'And even though it was incredible, you want to stick to that plan.'

She paused, trying to dilute the wave of pleasure from hearing that he'd thought it was incredible, too. 'That's right.'

'Any particular reason?'

Was he disappointed? Wasn't this the usual modus operandi for him—easy come, easy go?

'Seth.' She walked back to the bed and sat beside him, making the mistake of looking into his narrowed eyes. 'Last night was like having this incredibly rich dessert. Really decadent and delightful but if you have too much…it's not good for you. You know?'

He silently looked at her, then swiftly sat up. The sheet dropped low to his hips. She mentally screamed at herself not to look down—but her peripheral vision was feasting anyway and she could feel her flush blooming.

He grinned and slipped his hand to the back of her neck to pull her close. She didn't resist. This was the goodbye. This was absolutely the goodbye kiss. And, hell, he knew how to do it. His lips teased hers, his tongue tormenting with the promise of that sweet, carnal seduction all over again. She leaned closer, opened deeper, the roughness of his stubble sending delicious shivers down her spine. Passion, hunger, heat grew. She slid her hands wide over his shoulders and arms, celebrating his hot skin and the hard strength beneath. Her will weakened, almost dissolving completely in his fire.

He drew back, delight shining in his eyes and smile. 'How can too much of that *not* be good for you?'

She focused on regulating her breathing and restoring calm to her seriously overwrought system. 'Some things,' she said carefully, 'are best just left. You know?' This was definitely best left—for so many reasons. It had to stay as a fantasy. One that was finished.

Now both his smile and eyes widened as silently he studied her expression. She toughened up under the scrutiny—determined not to reveal her weakness. Determined to *beat* her weakness. He knew how to play it—he'd just tried already. So she didn't move a muscle as he stroked down her jaw with the back of a finger.

'You're very strong,' he murmured. 'What made you so strong?'

'Nothing very exciting.' She stood and walked away, trying to ignore the memories that ripped the scab from her heart and scalded her with hot, acidic guilt. They killed the temptation to succumb to him again. 'But once my mind is made up, it's made up.'

'Yeah,' he said, flopping back onto the pillow, his smile sounding. 'I can see you've got your game face on.'

She walked out of the bedroom before that mask slipped and revealed her true feelings. That stupid desire for *more*— the more that she'd never get from a guy like him. She wasn't going to waste time and emotional energy getting involved any further with someone who'd never offer what she really wanted. She'd done that once—spectacularly trashing her own life and hurting so many others. So why would she walk into another dead-end situation with her eyes wide open? There was nothing wrong with 'right now' but, as their 'now' had passed, there was no future.

He appeared, dressed but dishevelled. Looking just like the wild night he'd had and so gorgeous she went weak-kneed. Yes, there was that other problem—like suited like and Seth belonged to a different league from her. She didn't want to sit around waiting for the next woman to come along and outclass her.

'You want something to eat before you go?' She used the kitchen bench and the jug of hot coffee in her hand for defensive distance. Stopping herself from moving towards him.

That teasing smile tweaked his lips. 'No, I can see you're busy. I'll let you get on.'

She nodded, relieved he was now making this easy. Of course, he was a pro at everything women-related and clearly her calling time didn't bother him all that much. Another sign she was doing the right thing. 'Thanks for dinner and…everything,' she finished. So lame, she wanted to slither behind a rock somewhere.

'My pleasure. I had an amazing time,' he said easily.

But she heard bucketfuls of irony. She blushed—ridiculous considering everything they'd done. But he seemed so amused, and now the sunlight was streaming through the window the glare hurt her eyes. 'You won't say—'

'Just between us,' he interrupted carelessly. 'We both know that.'

'Great,' she said with masses more chirp than she felt. 'Well, thanks again.'

She saw the flash as his amusement deepened but then he turned. And that was it. He was out of the door before she got there to wave goodbye as a polite hostess ought to. She was frozen behind the bench, hot jug in hand, staring into the space he'd left behind.

Seth walked out of her house, got into his car and started driving. Out of earshot, his grin gave way to the full-body laugh he'd been holding back the last ten minutes. She wasn't used to the one-night scene or she'd have a more polished boot-him-out routine. She'd twisted up and iced over—spoiling her attempt to pull off a relaxed, sophisticated flick-off. But it was interesting that she wanted him out, and he believed that on one level she meant it when she said she didn't want more. But she did—he'd felt it when he'd kissed her. She'd responded so wonderfully, as she had throughout the night. She hadn't been exaggerating when she'd told him she wanted a good time, but she hadn't been completely selfish. She'd delighted in touching as much as she had in taking. Only, now her hedonistic moment had passed, she was back to the woman who said no.

Usually after a night or two of fun, Seth was ready to move on himself, but he and she definitely weren't yet done. Last night had merely been the preliminary and there'd be ten rounds in this ring. At least.

His phone beeped and he glanced at the screen. A drop of guilt slid like poison under his skin when he saw who the message was from. He was due to meet Andrew this afternoon and he'd promised he'd have a solution. He drew breath, telling himself that his selfish pleasure-seeking moment wouldn't have messed up the charity's chances for the following week. Lena would agree—in fact, Seth could use their tryst to his advantage, right? He could, of course, always buy their way into another sports club for the programme. If he had to he would, because he wasn't letting Andrew and the boys down. Except he wanted to be with the Knights next week, to be at the stadium as much as possible. Because he wanted Lena Kelly to have to say yes. Again. And then again.

He pulled in to his apartment and headed straight for the shower. He'd freshen up and then go in for the fight. Under the steaming jet of water he mulled over the possibilities, formulating a strategy that would see all his problems solved—an inspirational activity for the boys and Lena back in bed with him ASAP.

She might have cheated him out of the chase before, but it was all on now.

For the first time ever Lena was late to work—only by five minutes—but given she was usually there at least an hour early it was notable. This morning she'd stood so long in the shower it wasn't just her fingers and toes that had turned into prunes, but her face, as well. Or maybe the sour expression was because she was in an extremely bad mood—with herself.

She shouldn't have done it. Not that it was sleeping with him that she regretted, but her wistful aftermath. She wished she could have gone to breakfast with him at a café, wished she could have showered with him, wished she could have played more with him. Wished he'd want more from her. She wished she were a different person.

Yeah, the more she truly wished for, was from herself.

But while she was trying, some things weren't going to change, so there was no point in *wishing*. Instead she cleared her inbox, determined to finish even one job so she'd feel as if she'd accomplished something and was in control of her morning—and of herself. But it was an effort to keep her thoughts on task and she fiercely fought to focus. To help, she put on some music—letting the rhythmic beat be her lead. The one song on repeat became like white noise in the background, a cue for her brain to concentrate.

She finally got into the rhythm of it, her fingers typing and her head nodding in time, her emotions at ease, letting her brain work through each message. She paused, fingers above the keyboard as she framed the wording of her current email, and glanced away from the screen.

She jerked, doing a double take at the tall figure in her doorway.

Her heart leapt; she tried to suppress her gasp but all the effort did was make her breathless. 'What are you doing here?'

She had no idea how long he'd been standing there. She had no idea why he was standing there. But her whole body reacted, her numbed nerves screamed back to life—an instant inferno of surprise, embarrassment and that *uncontrollable* desire.

'Stalking you.' His smile was too easy.

Her heart galloped like trapped wild horses who'd just found a gap in the fence. Was he here to ask her out? She was so surprised and thrilled and flustered. 'I—I thought we agreed—'

'Don't worry, I was kidding,' he interrupted, walking across to her desk and taking the seat opposite in far too relaxed a fashion. 'There was a misunderstanding yesterday. I wasn't here to see Dion, I came to see you.'

'Me?' Suspicion sharply squeezed her heart 'Why?'

'We probably should have discussed this sooner, but I got…distracted.'

What should they have discussed? She swallowed, suddenly nervous. She refused to think about how he'd got distracted. She refused to think about how dazzling he looked in the tailored suit. How his slightly damp hair was rumpled, reflecting that hint of wicked playfulness she knew was a mere scratch below his surface. She refused to think about how much she wanted to touch him. *Now.*

He sat back in the chair, his gaze dropping to her scrupulously tidy desk. 'I'm involved with an organisation that helps at-risk youth. Teen boys mainly, who have had a couple of brushes with the law, who have high truancy levels. Kids who need some guidance and inspiration to stick to a straighter path.'

Lena's blood chilled as her heart shrank. She waited, knowing he was about to ask her for something and that it wasn't going to be personal. The man had an agenda. He'd had one the whole time.

His lashes lifted and his blue eyes were cool, his voice measured. He was clearly having no trouble focusing—a little fact that stung her already oversensitive nerves.

'Every few months we run a course,' he said. 'A mentoring programme.'

'What's this got to do with me—with the stadium?' she amended quickly. But she already knew where this was going and she was fighting the crushing feeling.

'We want to run the programme here—have the boys train alongside the team for a week. Let them see and understand what discipline, drive, dedication and hard work is. We have compulsory workshops in every course but we need permission to use the facilities here for it. And we need approval for our boys to attend training each day and to have the opportunity for some question-and-answer time with the team. The players are the inspiration factor for the boys. The kids need to see how hard those guys work, every day, and of course see what the rewards of extreme effort can be.'

She understood the aim immediately and knew the Silver Knights were a good example. They'd done that sort of thing before. Management encouraged the players themselves to continue with study so they had something to work towards when they finished playing professionally or if, worst case, they were injured and had their careers taken from them. They tried to help them build rounded lives and steer them through the pitfalls of temptation that fame and accolade brought. The rugby guys were driven and worked hard—hard enough to make dreams a reality. Some had come from childhoods of hardship. So, yes, most were inspirational for a lot of people. Of course some played around after hours but every single one was utterly determined and focused when it came to it—the game on the grass came first. Seth's request made total sense and was nothing new.

But Lena was battling bone-deep disappointment and bubbling anger. He should have told her about this yesterday. Instead he'd toyed with her. He'd let her make a total fool of herself.

'I have a presentation.' He pulled a flash drive from his pocket and placed it on her desk. 'Some slides and footage of the last few camps. It explains everything and only takes a few minutes to watch.'

She ignored it. 'When did you want to run this programme?'

'Next week.'

Her jaw dropped; she was stunned that he'd be that disorganised. 'Leaving it to the last minute, aren't you?'

He inclined his head and looked directly at her. 'It was scheduled for our usual place but that's become unavailable—fire gutted the main training room in the weekend. So I guess I'm throwing myself on your mercy.'

Mercy? Seth Walker had never needed anyone's mercy—he'd be the one to grant it.

'I can't be influenced by any personal—' she broke off, scrambling for an appropriate word '—connection we've had.'

'Of course.' He was totally smooth. 'I know that you wouldn't deny these boys this opportunity because of any awkwardness between us. Anyway, there isn't any awkwardness, is there?'

She was the one to study the desk then because she couldn't answer that. She wasn't feeling *awkward*, she was feeling insanely disappointed that he hadn't come to see her for *her*.

Of course he hadn't. And why should she mind when she'd told him it was over? But she totally minded. She wished her body had listened as well as he had.

'It's a good PR opportunity for the team, to be seen giving something back to the community, right?' he said.

'We have many good PR opportunities,' she answered curtly. 'The team already spends hours on community and charitable projects. Perhaps it's you who's really seeking the PR op?'

'I'm not in any of the pictures, nor is my company logo.' He grinned. 'I prefer to keep under the radar media wise. In fact my involvement with the programme is conditional on my *lack* of involvement with the publicity angle.'

Lena swallowed, knowing she was being backed into a corner.

'I spoke with Dion and, while he's happy for us to be at the stadium, you're the person who needs to let us have access to the team.' Seth's gaze speared her; he seemed to take up all her visual space.

'It's not me,' she denied. 'All I can do is put your request to management and get back to you.'

He leaned back in his seat, looking a lot as if he were a panther and she the hapless creature on whom he was about to pounce. 'But Dion said you were the key. If we get you onside it would basically be a done deal.'

If 'we' get her onside? *He* was the only one present—so it was if *he* got her 'onside'. Was this why he'd been so ready to accept her invitation last night? Had it been a case of sweetening her up so she'd say yes to this? Oh, now she was humiliated. Anger simmered, too.

'Nothing's a done deal,' she said, falling back on the icy armour she'd honed over the last eighteen months. 'I can make you no guarantees. You'll have to wait until I've reviewed the request and spoken with my superiors.' She stood, wanting this interview to be over so she could lick away the stings in private.

'Of course.' He followed suit and rose from his seat.

Politeness required she see him out. She'd failed to do that in her home this morning. Now she was determined to be *nothing* but professional—pride dictated it. But it was in stony silence that she walked towards her door.

'Don't come out to the lift. I'm sure you're very busy.' He smiled—too intimately.

She lifted her chin. 'It's no problem.'

His grin flashed wider as if he didn't believe her. 'Lena—' he stopped just inside her doorway '—just so you know, I don't prostitute myself.' He leaned closer, spoke in an all-out purr. 'Not even for a good cause.'

She couldn't move.

'What happened last night was between us and has nothing to do with this.' Now he bit.

'What happened last night is finished,' she said firmly.

'You think?' His lashes dropped; she could feel the sweep of his gaze down her skin as if it were the stroke of his finger. 'Who are you trying to convince—me or you?'

Oh, he was arrogant and she had the urge to best him somehow.

'Because, in case you hadn't figured it out already,' he continued softly, 'you can ask me to dine on you again any time you like.'

Dine *on* her? Heat flared in her cheeks over the crudity of his comment. And the veracity: she *had* asked, more than once, and he'd licked every inch of her body—inside and out. Just as she'd sucked the proof of pleasure out of him. Her skin burned, not just from anger but also attraction—still that insane attraction to his physicality. And his amusement. For once more laughter sparkled in the depths of his blue eyes, inviting her to laugh with him. Except she couldn't. She couldn't move, speak, think.…

It took her catatonic brain long enough to realise she was panting. She snapped out of it, marched back to her desk and swiped up the flash drive—to do *something* with her damp, shaking, desperate hands. 'I'll take a look and get back to you.'

'Here's my card.' Remaining where he was, he held it out—so she had to walk back towards him to get it. 'I forgot to give you my details this morning.'

She had his every detail imprinted on her body. She could still feel his weight, still see the shades of tan on his skin, the whirls of hair on his chest—the arrowing down to his fantastic masculinity. She knew every intimate detail already; she didn't need more.

She took the card by a corner edge and quickly moved to the open door to avoid any closer contact. 'I'll be in touch,' she said brusquely.

He nodded—too casually—and sent her a brilliant smile. 'I really do appreciate your time, Lena.'

She turned her back on him and gritted her teeth to hold in the snarl of pure frustration. But she couldn't say no to his request and he knew it. The team tried to agree to most team-access requests—especially if youth or children were involved. She had to treat this proposal as she would any other—because if their night together ever became public knowledge it would look so dodgy. In truth it looked dodgy either way.

Damn Seth for putting her in this position. He should have been honest with her in the first place. She ground her teeth harder still. Men never were honest—not until they'd got what they wanted. She tossed the flash drive onto the desk and sat down to fire off the relevant emails. Yes, she'd recommend this to management, but only because there was no reason not to and because Dion had already given permission for them to be on-site. It was off-season, the boys were only playing a couple of friendlies in the next fortnight, there was none of the cloak-and-dagger secret-training stuff that happened around finals time.

But while she'd say yes, she'd avoid the pitch completely next week. She'd catch up on the filing or something so she wouldn't even have to see him. She swallowed her disappointment and stoked her small pocket of pride. She had no intention of having to deal with him direct ever again.

CHAPTER SIX

THE next morning Lena cleared her emails. It was all organised. She'd had confirmation messages from Andrew, the social worker for the charity. Nothing from Seth himself. Of course not—he'd got what he wanted already. Grimacing, she picked up the box of sponsorship goodies that had arrived for the totally spoilt team. She'd leave them in their lockers; the boys should be on the pitch already, ten minutes into training.

'Coming through!' she called just in case, but the change room was silent and empty. She started unloading the box, chuckling when she saw that it was the two best-looking stars of the team who had the specially wrapped, larger freebie packs.

Footsteps sounded behind her and she turned, expecting it to be one of the guys. It was a guy, all right. She stared at the bare chest, instantly recognising and responding to the dusting of dark hair and defined pecs and abs. It hadn't been baby oil that had made this chest gleam the last time she'd seen it; it had been sweat and wet—from her lips and tongue.

It took all her willpower not to lick her lips now, and far too many seconds before she could drag her gaze upwards. The silence, for all that time, said it all.

'What are you doing here?' she finally asked, trying not

to let her streaming excitement sound, but he had to be able to hear her heart battering her rib cage.

'What does it look like?' Eyes dancing, he took for ever to slip his tee shirt over his head. 'I'm doing a training session with the team. I need to know what to prepare the boys for next week.'

*'What?'* Horrified, she glared at him. 'That's not a good idea.'

'Why not?'

'Because…' She paused. Because he'd probably get killed—but how did she say that without sounding too concerned? 'Can you afford the dental work?' she eventually spat.

'So little faith?' Good humour beamed from his face. She knew he was enjoying her OTT reaction.

'You're not a professional rugby player. Those guys are demons.' Oh, hell, she sounded pathetic.

'Why, Lena—' he put his hand to his chest '—you care about what happens to me?'

'I wouldn't like to see *anyone* permanently paralysed,' she corrected him bluntly.

'Your concern for my welfare is very sweet, but I've no intention of being pulverised.'

On that pitch he wasn't going to have the choice. The Knights were the best team in the country. Fighting machines who showed no mercy. Ever.

Without realising, she followed him out of the change room into the tunnel and towards the pitch. 'Why are you doing this?'

'Well, there are a couple of reasons. I do need to prep for my boys.' He stopped right at the end of the tunnel and faced her. 'But I've also got energy to burn. More than a little frustration. Ice-cold showers aren't enough.'

His words torched Lena's cheeks. She clamped her jaw,

trying to ignore the flames licking deep inside her, too. Had he guessed she'd been having like three ice showers a day?

'Besides,' he continued easily, 'I've always wanted to play on this pitch.'

'This is some childhood fantasy?' What was it with these guys?

'Why not?' His smile was unrepentant and infuriatingly irresistible. 'I never played rugby as a boy, had a couple of part-time jobs and couldn't make the training sessions at school. So here I am, fulfilling that youthful ambition.'

'So your unholy desire to make truckloads of money began right when you were a kid?'

Her sarky comeback killed the smile in his eyes, leaving them colder than she'd ever seen them. 'Like most people, I like to eat. And in order to do that on a reasonably regular basis, I had to work.'

Lena swallowed, lost for words and suddenly sorry.

'We didn't all have the perfect upbringing with the piano and tennis lessons and home-baked biscuits in our lunch boxes,' he tossed, stepping out onto the grass.

'Seth—' Lena called after him, now angry, too, because he was as wrong as she'd been.

He turned and glared, defiance flaming in his eyes. 'Here's the thing, Lena. You don't know me very well. And you certainly don't know how determined I can be.'

His chin lifted as he jogged to join in the warm-up drills. Open-mouthed, Lena watched. *Determined?* About what she thought he meant? He turned his head, flashing another look at her.

Oh, yes, he did mean that—because that defiance was desire drenched. Stupidly, all she could wonder then was whether he had a mouth guard. Irresistibly she was drawn to the rail. Dion was lounging against it, yapping into his mobile phone. She didn't want to watch the carnage, but her body wasn't listening to her brain. When it came to Seth, her body refused to hear sense.

'Hey!' A few of the guys grinned and high-fived Seth.

A few others shivered, and drew away from him as if they were afraid.

'Don't be too hard on us, bro. We don't wanna see any of your KO moves out here.'

Seth just grinned. Lena frowned. What were they talking about?

The start-up drills were easy—running, ball skills, none of the blood-splattering tackles to begin with, but it would only be a matter of time. She watched him—black shorts, grey tee shirt. Lean, fit, hard. Edible. But not a rugby professional.

She gripped the rail tightly, trying to get a grip on the adrenaline coursing through her, trying to lose the fear factor.

'You didn't want to get out there, too?' she asked Dion when he put the phone into his pocket. If it was slam-the-amateur hour, then shouldn't he be getting bloodied, as well?

'Hell, no, I'd only play against Seth in a non-contact sport like chess or something. Even then, he'd clean me up.'

Really? If she weren't feeling so anxious she'd roll her eyes. But they were glued to Seth's sleek physique. He was fast and fully holding his own; she'd easily lose him in the mix. 'Is Gabe in?' she asked breathlessly. She'd feel better knowing the team doctor was on-site.

Dion chuckled. 'Seth's not going to need him, if that's what you're thinking. I think the boys are more afraid of him than he is of them.'

Amazingly that outlandish comment seemed to be accurate. The team were throwing cautious looks his way, but that was probably because they were afraid of hurting him or something. Except it didn't look like that would happen. How *did* a guy who bought and sold buildings end up with such sharp muscles? How come his abs were more defined than most of the other guys'? How come he wasn't breathless and panting after all those sprints? Some of the locks looked as if they were hitting their cardio limit already but Seth was still smiling. And the warm-up was working for her as much as for those locks, because all she could think about was his body pouring all that power into hers.

'Why would they be afraid of him?' Lena asked, half panting herself.

'Because he has a killer left hook. In his time he KO'd more opponents than anyone else in his division.'

KO'd as in *knocked out*? 'You mean he's a boxer?'

'Yeah.' Dion answered as if he was amazed she didn't know that. 'He was a national amateur champ.'

No way. Seth wasn't a boxer. Where were the battle scars? Where was the bump in the nose from the repeated breaks? His face was far too perfect. She stared at him as she processed. *Boxing?* It was even more violent than rugby.

So he really was a fighter. No wonder he had such a fit body. As a rule she loathed the sport—loathed the violence. Only, now she felt a rush of liquid heat at the thought of him engaged in something so overtly masculine—that raw determination to channel untamed aggression. She shivered. Wasn't the aim to physically hurt another and assert dominance primitive and barbaric?

Yet when Seth had dominated her, when he'd used his body to torment hers, it had been with tenderness. Ferocious passion, yes—but also infinite tenderness.

The dichotomy intrigued and inflamed her. There was greater complexity to the man than she'd realised and she was so curious. Why had he got into boxing? Why was he working with these at-risk youth? He hadn't been exaggerating when he'd said he wasn't after promo ops. She'd checked his website yesterday and there was nothing personal about him on there. The first hits on a quick Google search had been pictures of him on the town with beautiful women and had been so depressing she'd shut down the search instantly.

She shoved the questions away now, too. Curiosity got cats into serious trouble, after all. She turned and went to hide in her office. Organising her in-tray, she counted the seconds down until she figured it was safe to go back down to the change room and sort the rest of the stuff she'd abandoned. The boys should have finished and cleared out—they had a session with the dietician on a Thursday.

'Coming through!' she called regardless, her voice echoing in the empty room.

'I hoped I'd see you again.' He stepped round the corner.

Okay, so the room wasn't quite empty. And he hadn't changed, still hot and sweaty, his body looking all the more powerful.

'I jogged round the pitch a few more times after training had ended,' he answered her unspoken question. 'I'm still suffering from more energy than I know what to do with.'

She glanced up to his face, just for a second. But that second morphed into an endless moment because the expression in his eyes entranced her. It was that total focus, the look that made her feel as if there were nothing and no one else in the world but her. She tried to break free but it was impossible. Lust, she reminded herself, just lust. A hormonal mix headier than most—okay, deadly. But lust meant nothing. This could *be* nothing.

His tee shirt clung to his breadth, his skin gleamed, his chest rose and fell faster than usual. He was steaming hot. And she was dying of attraction. She had to kill it.

'You need a shower,' she said roughly. But she needed one more.

All Seth could think about was hauling her into the shower with him. Yeah, the whole point of the exercise this morning was purely to see her again—not play rugby. He wasn't really a team-sports guy. He preferred one-to-one challenges. Like this. He'd spent hours wondering what she'd be wearing when he saw her next and it was every bit as gorgeous as he'd fantasised. He'd seen the millions of dresses in her wardrobe when she'd opened it yesterday morning. He loved the way they emphasised her shape, loved the fantasy of lifting her skirt and having easy access. Today she wore emerald green. It would look even better wet.

Deliberately he stepped closer, his intent sharpening when she didn't step back. He watched for a blush or something—anything—to clue him in to her thoughts. He hoped they were as rabid as his were. But she was one hell of a blank slate and the poker fantasy came back at the worst possible moment.

'Can you really leave it at just one night?' The question slid out of him—and wasn't at all an example of the cool way he'd planned to play it.

Her brows lifted. 'One night was all I needed.'

Never. 'What about what I needed?'

'Oh, Seth,' she answered slowly. 'You've got a zillion other options to get your needs met.'

True, but that wasn't the point. 'Maybe I don't want other options. I want you to meet my needs.' He frowned, struck by a nightmare thought. 'Have you got other options?'

'No,' she snapped right back. 'But maybe I don't have the same level of need as you.'

He laughed—hard—before thinking better of it. 'No, we both know your needs are way greater than mine.'

Her jaw became more defined, her chin pointier. 'You've got the wrong impression.'

'I don't think so.'

She might be gritting her teeth and his balls ought to be frozen by the dry ice steaming from her eyes, but he was committed now. He saw her bite harder on her lip.

'Relax, Lena.' He took her hand and smoothed his fingers across her cold knuckles. 'Tense doesn't suit you.' He knew what did.

'I'm not tense.'

Her pulse slammed into his fingertips, fast and furious. Her wanting—her *not* wanting to want. He didn't really want to want her quite like this, either, but he wasn't as into denial as she was. Surely she knew if they gave into it, it would go away. It always did. He glanced down and saw she'd curled one foot around her other leg, so she was standing in a weird flamingo kind of way. Totally closed off, with her toes curled in the ends of her sandals. Toe curling was a good sign, wasn't it? Toe curling meant she was holding something back. Satisfaction made him smirk but she saw and jerked her wrist free.

'You know, you're supposed to be highly intelligent, but the most boneheaded rugby boy has got it before you. I'm saying no.'

'I am highly intelligent,' he answered patiently. 'So I can see straight through what you're trying to do.'

'Oh, what do you think that is?'

'You're playing me, keeping me dangling on your string.'

'You think I want you on my string?' she muttered. 'Your arrogance is something else.'

'Yeah, but I'm right. Women like to manipulate. You play hardest to get when you want it most, as if somehow it's wrong to want it so badly and putting up a fight makes it more acceptable.' He moved closer, needing to be near. 'But there's something about a woman who's honest about wanting it, and who wants it as much as I do. Be honest with me again, Lena.'

'You're wrong,' she said firmly, her ice-chipped eyes unwavering. 'Not all women play those kinds of games. I don't. I mean what I say.'

'But a massive part of you doesn't want to say it.' Her toe curling was giving it away. He hoped.

'You think?' She glared at him, her ice dissolving in anger. 'You're actually a no-means-yes, take-it-willing-or-not brute?'

'You can try to be as insulting as you like but it isn't going to work.' He grinned. 'You can't manipulate me into getting angry and walking away.' He'd literally fought to learn to control his emotions—it took a hell of a lot for him to give way to anger now. And he was miles off angry at the moment, more like amused. Her lashes lowered and he waited expectantly, eager to see her next move.

'It's all about the game for you, isn't it?' She peeped a look back up.

He smiled because she couldn't resist that little look. And, yeah, she had his number, but he'd get hers, too. He'd tease it out. 'I don't think you can deny this, Lena. You were so hot the other day you exploded at first touch. How long had you been on the boil?' He angled his head, leaning closer, deliberately trying to bait her because it was working. 'I don't actually think it's me. Clearly working around all this testosterone gets you het up and after a while your safety valve blows. Best it blows with someone like me rather than one of those boys, though, right? You wouldn't want to get messy in the workplace, would you?'

She went pale. Seth's radar zeroed in. Oh, that was interesting—was that why she was so stand-offish with the team? She'd once had a messy office affair? His curiosity raged. Yeah, there was the thing. This wasn't just about getting her back into bed; he wanted to know all about her. Most of all he wanted to know what else would make her laugh.

Lena drew breath and forced history back to the past. Seth thought she'd been horny from hanging with the rugby guys? He was crazy. Those boys were beautiful, but they didn't light her fire. It was all him. Something in him called to her, something she feared was more than skin deep. But she was happy to let him keep his wholly wrong idea. The sass only Seth sparked bubbled up and she leaned forward, reckless. 'It's a once-a-year thing,' she whispered. 'Can you hang on that long?'

'Once a year?' He laughed, predatory sharpness defining his features once more. 'You haven't a hope in lasting that this time. You're still thermonuclear.'

She pulled back, putting both feet down to stand her ground. 'And you're delusional.'

'No.' He shook his head slowly. His lashes lifted and the azure-blue eyes gleamed at her thoughtfully. 'What I am is honoured.'

'I'm sorry?' He'd lost her totally now.

'An annual event *at most,*' he said, utterly serious. 'Given you were worried you'd forgotten how, I'm honoured that you picked me the other night. And as it was such a rare experience for you, I take it to be a real privilege. And a compliment.'

She ground her teeth. 'The other day you were making out like I was in here getting the entire team off.'

He nodded. 'Amazing how wrong that first impression was, huh?' He sidled closer with a snaky smile. 'What was your first impression of me?'

'That you're an arrogant jerk.'

'See?' He beamed widely. '*So* wrong.'

She stared at him for a second and then couldn't help but laugh. Her chuckle deepened as the tension eased. It felt good. 'You're…you're…'

'Ready when you are,' he quipped. 'Come on, let's get out of here.'

She kept shaking her head but couldn't pull back her smile. 'Incorrigible. Unrepentant. *Impossible*. Please give up.' She really meant that.

'I can't believe you're asking me to.' He dropped his joking manner and moved back in on her, closer than before.

Her skin tingled, threatening to burst all over with goose bumps. Oh, he was good. Temptation shook her foundations.

'Yes,' he whispered, stepping closer and holding her gaze captive.

Was he saying yes for the both of them?

She swallowed, but she couldn't stop her honesty. 'Okay, I won't deny I'm attracted to you. But it's more intelligent to walk away.' And she was so determined to do the intelligent thing, the right thing for her this time.

'How can that possibly be more intelligent? You know it'll be good.'

'I told you.' Her chest ached while her belly burned. 'Too much of a good thing leaves you feeling bad.'

'So we won't have too much, then.' He shrugged. 'Just a little more.'

It wouldn't work that way for her. She'd fall quickly, deeply, uselessly. It would take nothing to fall hard for Seth.

'Look at me,' he said quietly, but with an undertone that made her nerves screech. 'Just for a second.'

Seth really needed to see into her eyes to try to fathom what she was thinking. Except when he did he still had no bloody idea.

'I don't want to have a fling with you,' she said softly.

He paused, knew he had to be honest with her. 'Lena, I'm a lifetime off marriage.'

Her eyes flashed. 'I'm not exactly painting the nursery, either.'

'Okay, but let me tell you why I'm not.'

'You want to share your sob story to win me over? Play on my emotional feminine side? Butter me up so I say yes?'

Her sudden cynicism silenced him for a second—someone had to have played a real sob story on her in the past. 'No, I just want you to understand where I'm coming from.' Mainly because he wanted to know what *her* story was and he figured if he shared, she'd share. It usually worked that way. Once he understood the reason for the reluctance, he could see her through it. Carefree didn't mean careless, after all. He only wanted nice, light, naughty fun for both of them. And while she might sound as if she wasn't interested, she was all eyes and ears.

He put it lightly. 'Look, my parents divorced in one terrible mess. Put me off for life.'

'How convenient for you to have an emotional reason for not committing,' she said sarcastically.

He bit back a laughing grunt. She had no idea of the reality. That divorce had been too long in coming—months of bitterness and betrayal. Months of his mother trying to make it work. Months of him trying to be the model son.

'Fortunately I was spared a nasty custody battle,' he said drily. Yeah, there'd been a total *lack* of custody battle. The father he'd once been dumb enough to idolise had walked out and never looked back. Too busy with his new family to be interested. His mother had been devastated and Seth hadn't been enough to help her. And that made it suck all the more. All that hideous turbulence combined with teen displacement had seen his anger threaten to screw his life completely. Control had come in isolation, with him literally fighting it out. And he'd learned what he needed to succeed—just his emotionally unencumbered self.

He forced himself to breathe, to keep the flippant tone, to fast-forward. 'But of course I do have an evil ex.'

'Of course you have an evil ex. Do tell,' she anti-invited, saccharine sweet. There was no softening her.

'First year uni. Medicine. I scored the girlfriend that all the guys wanted. The hostel hottie.'

Her eyes narrowed; he half hoped the green was glowing deeper from jealousy.

'But then I started the pizza thing. I'd designed the tee shirts for the delivery guys to wear and they turned out to be as popular as the pizzas. I knew I had a chance at something, so I dropped out to pursue it full-time. According to her I was going to be a loser like my dad—who incidentally *was* a total loser.' For a second his mood darkened.

'And her attitude only motivated you all the more?'

He managed a smile. 'Of course.' She'd laughed, then grown scornful. There'd been no attempt to understand, no belief in *him*. No, he very quickly learned that belief had to come from your*self*, success from your*self*, happiness from your*self*. Dependence on others didn't get you anywhere. Dependence on others got you hurt—check out Exhibit A, his mother. She'd relied on having a husband and kids to be happy. But her husband had left and she only had the one kid. He hadn't been enough. Still couldn't do enough. He hadn't been enough for the girlfriend, either—not once he'd lost the status of being the top student in his med class.

'No doubt she lived to regret her decision?' Lena batted her lashes, still sarcasm personified.

Yeah, she wasn't taking his confidences terribly seriously. But what had happened had really sucked and stupidly still bothered him—well, to a degree. 'She started dating my arch rival in med. Until I dropped out, he and

I had been competing for class honours. He won both the first-year prize and her. But when the marriage faltered she looked me up.'

By then he was a multimillionaire and had more status and success than any general practitioner. It was only the status and success that had attracted her.

'Did you have an affair?' Lena was looking at the floor now.

Seth had been angry at the invitation. His ex had no problem with infidelity, but he did. 'No, and even when she was divorced I still said no. I don't repeat my mistakes.' He'd known what it was she'd wanted—the money and status, not actually him.

'And since then you've done the dumping, right?'

He'd ended every fling—all except for Lena Kelly.

'Is that why you're here now?' she asked sharply. 'Because I said no?'

'No.' He should have seen she'd leap to that conclusion. 'I'm here because I'm honest enough to admit I want to be with you again.'

'It's just sex.'

'Not *just* sex, fantastic sex.' And he had the sinking feeling that wasn't all it was. The desire to be near her, to know her, was more than sexual. He studied her blank expression. 'So has my sob story scored your sympathy?'

'This all happened, what, a decade or so ago and you're still not over it?'

Ouch. He chuckled. 'You know how it is, the first cut's deep.' And you were landed with the parent dramas for life. He might be able to forget his father now, but his mother still frustrated the hell out of him. He still couldn't help her the way he wanted to be able to.

Lena was really trying to diminish the effect of his opening up to her. It wasn't that much of a sob story, right? Loads of people had parental issues and ex issues. She had them herself. 'You really want my sympathy?'

'Right now I'll take whatever I can get. Are you going to try to save my scarred heart?'

'I have enough awareness of my limitations to know that's not possible,' she said with heartfelt honesty. 'Besides, I'm not convinced you actually have a heart. I think what you have is an overblown need to win. You don't like me calling time ahead of you.'

'Well, you have to agree you did it prematurely.' He grinned. 'Why did you? What's made you such a scaredy cat?'

'I'm not scared, I'm being sensible.'

'Sensible doesn't suit you.' His voice dropped. 'Your beauty glows when you laugh and when you're reckless.'

'The lines won't work.' Except they were and now she was desperately trying not to dwell on the tantalising information she'd just learned, but in truth examining every salient fact. So his parents had split, so he had a witch ex-girlfriend. And dropping out of med school to make pizza and print tee shirts with pithy slogans did seem a random path—one that only Seth could make succeed.

She wasn't supposed to have learned anything more about him. She wasn't supposed to have become any more curious. He was supposed to have walked out of her life yesterday—for good. Only, now she was beyond intrigued. And the more she knew, the more she wanted. That delicious melting feeling immobilised her. He was watching, smiling, and she knew he knew.

'You really don't want me to kiss you again?'

He was so close her skin was doing the alternate sizzle-then-tingle thing.

'You don't want me to slide my hand like this?' To her waist, to draw her close.

She dug in her toes, trying to hang on to the last scrap of sanity she had left. And then, thank goodness, she remembered.

'You need to step back,' she whispered jerkily. 'There's a camera in here.'

Seth froze, then glanced up at the ceiling and round the walls. 'In the *change room*?'

'The half-time cam for the at-home audience. The guys know where it's placed so they don't change in front of it. But we're centre-screen right now.'

He spotted it, on the wall beside them. 'Is it filming?' He was horrified they had a camera in here.

'Not something I'm risking.' She had her distance back now, and she was growing it—literally.

'Not willing to risk much, are you?' Seth called after her as she scampered off. Fists clenched, he thought about hitting the wall, but it was concrete and he wasn't *that* stupid. Damn the camera.

Privacy was important to him. But breaking through her barriers had been more important. So he'd spilled some details he rarely shared— in the hope she'd confide something in return. Only, she hadn't. Lena Kelly wasn't like other women. She was saying no, but she still wanted him. That had never happened before. And he sure as hell didn't want to be haunted by her, which right now he was.

He wondered what the mess was she'd landed herself in. It had to have been a big one. He knew the wounded look and he'd seen those shadows pass in her eyes a few times. As a rule he avoided bruised women—they had vampiric emotional needs and he didn't do angst or drama. Didn't have the resources within him. Not for anyone. Better to play light and leave the needy alone. But he wanted Lena. He wanted the sparkle he'd seen more often in those same beautiful eyes. He wanted the laughter in his arms again.

There had to be a way of making it impossible for her to say no for much longer, but, short of parading round half-naked like some rent boy, he really didn't know how he was going to manage it.

It would be simpler if he found someone else, but he had the feeling no other woman would be remotely interesting until he understood all there was to Lena. And had her every which way and back again. He was so on her leash and she was jerking him hard. She was proving better than he at this despite not being anywhere near as much of a player.

Breathing hard, he flicked the shower to freezing and gritted his teeth. His muscles twitched, eager to release pent-up energy as if the two hours' hard-out training had never happened. Dressed, no less frustrated, he thudded up the stairs to Dion's office. Dion glanced up from his computer and a way-too-amused look crossed his face.

'She smacked you down,' Dion said.

Seth shrugged.

'Don't take it personally,' Dion soothed evilly. 'It's happened to all of us.'

'You asked her out?' That really didn't help his mood.

Dion just grinned and swivelled his chair to stare out of the window.

'You're her boss.' Annoyance tainted his supposedly lazy drawl.

'Not technically,' Dion mused. 'I'm here courtesy of the council, she's employed by the team management.'

'Dion.' Seth glowered. 'That doesn't make it any better.'

'Don't get steamed.' Dion raised his hands into the surrender position and laughed, spinning back to face him. 'I didn't, okay? I'm not into sexual harassment or power plays.'

'Yet you have those cheerleader girls in the tiniest outfits,' Seth muttered, not ready to laugh yet.

'And the rugby guys are all but naked in the calendar.' Dion shook his head. 'Lena is all yours, but if she doesn't want you, she doesn't want you, and I've never seen her change her mind. You might just have to deal with failure for once.'

Seth didn't know the meaning of the word. And he had no intention of finding it out now.

## CHAPTER SEVEN

FOR the first half of Monday morning Lena managed to avoid them altogether. They'd arrived, she'd heard the voices; if she went to look out of the floor-to-ceiling windows in the corridor she'd be able to see them on the field. But she kept herself busy buried behind paper. Okay, she was forcing herself to stay there—and the second hand on the clock was ticking too slowly. Eventually, however, her shrieking curiosity could no longer be ignored. She walked down to the change rooms—didn't go into them, though, went straight along the tunnel that led to the pitch instead.

The Knights were working one half of it, pacing through their usual drills. On the other half was some really tall lanky guy, a disparate tribe of teens and the ultra-fit one in the familiar tee shirt and shorts. Seth was calling the play, making them sweat. But also, she saw in less than six seconds, making them laugh.

She couldn't help lingering to watch the interaction between him and the boys. The tall guy was clearly the sidekick, because he was the one doing the big ups and support shouts, while Seth was the one pushing the boys to work. She knew from reading their planned schedule that it wouldn't all be fun on the footie field. They had workshops on all kinds of topics—from drugs and alcohol, to anger management, to basic reading and writing.

She leaned against the rail, couldn't help tracking that one player. And he knew it. Even from fifty feet away she felt it when his attention shot to her. Her body temp lifted as hormones surged. Her heart was pounding as fast as those boys' ones were and she didn't have the exercise excuse for it. Eventually the two groups were pulled together and re-split so they could play a mini-game. Youth and professional. But she watched the one who refused to fit into any category. Lena turned; she'd be stuck here all day achieving nothing if she didn't force her feet to move. It wasn't okay to stand on the sideline and drool—she *wasn't* a groupie, remember?

Ten minutes later she was in the change room sorting the latest box of PR goodies when she heard the shouting. She ran back down the tunnel, nearly bumping into a rookie player sprinting the other way. Quickly she scanned the field. But it wasn't Seth or any of his boys who was down. The Knights were gathered into a loose circle—one of their own sprawled on the ground. Seth stood on the edge of the group. Footsteps thudded past, beating faster than Lena's galloping heart. Gabe moved swiftly across the close-cropped grass, kit bag in hand, while the player who'd fetched him jogged alongside.

But that player wasn't the rookie she'd passed in the corridor. Suddenly Lena remembered that kid's pale face as he'd run. No prizes for guessing who'd been on top in the tackle. Relief hit. She was so thankful it hadn't been one of Seth's boys who'd been involved. But then she remembered the recent history of the rookie who had. Quickly she turned back into the tunnel; twenty seconds later she found him, fists clenched, as he leaned against the wall just outside the change room. He didn't say anything as she neared, didn't look up, didn't move.

She touched his shoulder lightly. 'It's okay,' she said firmly. 'Gabe's with him.'

She felt his flinch and then his grip on himself tightened.

'I didn't mean to…' Beneath his fierce expression she saw his devastation.

'Of course you didn't.' She wished one of the guys would come—like now. Because this kid had been in a game before where another young up-and-comer had ended up with broken bones and smashed dreams and she didn't know if she was saying the right thing.

'You know they want players with passion,' she tried anyway. 'They want guys who put everything they have into it. Risk comes with that. Accidents happen.'

'I don't want to kill another guy's career.'

'You won't have.' At least, she hoped not. 'You're a great player. They believe in you. Your team-mates believe in you.' Anxiously she looked into his face, wishing she could reassure him. 'I believe in you. And your job is to get back out there. They need you to be the force you are.'

'Lena's right, mate.' The assistant coach spoke from behind her. 'He's fine. Bit groggy but nothing that can't be fixed. You know it was a clean tackle.'

Thank goodness they were there at last—the assistant coach and Ty. She quickly raised her brows at the captain and he winked. She breathed a sigh of relief. 'Talk to Coach and get back out there,' she said to the rookie as she moved away. 'Train hard.'

'Thanks, Lena,' the kid called gruffly as she walked back out towards the pitch.

Only, her adrenaline levels didn't dim, because Seth was at the end of the tunnel.

'You really know the history of them all, don't you?' he said quietly as she neared.

So he'd been listening in.

'Sure,' she answered on auto, trying to keep her eyes on the players who were back into training and nowhere near Seth. Because he was even more bone-melting masculine with his just-worked-out glow on. 'It's helpful when I do the PR spin on the tours. People like to know facts and figures.'

'We sure do,' he murmured lightly. 'But he's okay? Because the other guy's fine.'

She glanced, unable to resist the concerned note in his voice. Big mistake. In a microsecond of sharing the same airspace as him again, she was back to the wildly wanting woman of a week ago. She couldn't believe it. Surely sex was supposed to shred all the tension? Surely once you'd gorged on the cake you didn't want any more? It wasn't supposed to leave you hungrier than ever.

'I think so.' Lena forced her answer, but she was drowning in his blue eyes and she started babbling, 'He's got huge power, but he's still learning how to handle it. He'll end up an amazing player. Are your boys okay?'

'A bit subdued.'

'It's probably no bad thing for them to see the reality of injury.'

Lena jumped at the foreign voice. Turning, she realised the tall lanky guy was standing beside them. She'd been so busy staring at Seth she hadn't noticed.

'Lena, this is Andrew, the boys' social worker.' Seth introduced her with a knowing grin.

Embarrassed, she shook his hand.

'I heard you talking to him,' Andrew said. 'It'd be great if you could talk to our boys, too.'

'Don't mind Andrew's directness.' Seth chuckled. 'He's shameless about asking for what he wants.'

Lena knew someone far more shameless and she flashed him a look telling him so.

Andrew seemed to miss the undertone as he went on with

his query—all genuine enthusiasm. 'It would be great to give them an insight into the PR stuff that you expect from the team, how you curb their behaviour.'

'Some players' behaviour is impossible to curb,' Lena said, sending Seth another charged look before turning a softer smile to Andrew. 'But if you think it would be of interest, of course I will.'

Immediately after that she retreated to her upstairs domain, determinedly not looking out of the window at all for the next four hours. Wishing she could kill the desire to gawp at the gorgeous one all day. Wishing she'd never agreed to his presence here. But then, when the sun had passed the zenith and was on its way down, she heard it— the music.

Oh, no. She spun away from her desk and stood in the one swift movement, striding straight out to the corridor and out of one of the doors leading to the second-level seating of the stadium. Her high heels echoed as she moved down the concrete steps to the edge of the railing from where she had a fantastic view of the field. She stared—hard—and told herself she was *not* jealous.

But there was not one, not two, not even a mere three. There were five of them around him already. In their skimpy skirts with their legs up to their armpits and their hair down to their tiny little waists.

Just as Contez Stadium was home to the Silver Knights, it was also home to the Silver Blades—the dancers who entertained the crowds before the game and during the interval. And Lena had completely forgotten that Monday afternoon was their on-pitch practice session.

She knew a few of them. Most were students. Most were lovely. All were completely gorgeous—glossy, slim, sexy. Amazingly flexible, too. She tried very hard not to care about the flock currently hanging on Seth's every word as he stood encircled by them. She tried very hard not to glare. She wasn't interested in what he did with any or indeed all five of them. Who was she to judge? After all, she'd thrown herself at him, too. By rights all women should get to experience what she had a week ago.

Now she felt sick.

He glanced up to where she stood at the front of the stand and gave her a huge grin and an oversized wink. She froze, wanting to turn and storm off, only not wanting to be so damn obvious. But then, with a few words and a devilish smile, he extricated himself from the bevy of gorgeous-nesses. She remained frozen, watching as he crossed the grass and then walked up the steps, effortlessly swinging up and over the railing to where she stood like an ice sculpture.

'I see you've found the way to have your needs met.' She couldn't resist baiting.

His expression remained bland. 'Well, I do love women who don't try to hide what they want.'

She flushed but fought on anyway. 'Actually, not all women need a man.' She wanted to cut him down.

'No? You've got Ben Wa balls in and having orgasms every other second?'

Her mouth dropped. She snapped it shut again as his eyes sparked—daring her. His boys had gone and he was back to being as unsubtle as she'd been when they first met. The images flooding her head, the feelings flooding her body, were so not helping with getting her frost back.

'You don't need them,' he teased, not dropping the seduc-tive assault. 'You know I do a better job.'

'You—' She gulped.

'Your eyes give it all away,' he taunted gently. 'You haven't been able to take them off me.'

'I'm amazed you could notice anything past all that

cleavage,' she said cattily. Too inflamed to care about what she was revealing in the process.

'You're jealous as hell and you can't hide it.'

'You can sleep with who you like, it's none of my business. I really don't care.' She glared at the grass, pointedly *not* looking at him.

'Protesting too much.' He shook his head. 'And those poor young dancers. They're not the kind to take a guy home and do him over within ten minutes of talking to him.'

Her head whipped as she scowled at him, her frost snapping back. 'What do you mean, not the kind? As in some easy tart?'

He laughed—but his blue eyes intensified. 'We both know you're anything but easy.'

'That's right.' She batted out her words, all bravado. 'I'm way too difficult for you.'

'I actually think you might be right on that.' He grinned. 'You stand up to me.' He broke every social rule—moving too close, too quick, until he stood a mere millimetre away from her. 'I really like it how you don't back away.'

Well, that was only because she'd locked her knees tight to stop the jelly feeling in her thighs, so as a result she couldn't take a single step. 'You don't think it's rude to invade my personal space?'

'If you were uncomfortable with it you'd move.'

'Over the railing in these shoes?' she asked sarcastically.

The Cheshire cat's grin just went wider. Okay, so the railing was a good metre away and she could get around him if she wanted.

He bent and breathed in her ear. 'Fact is you like me this close.'

She did. She also liked the way his shorts wrapped close around his thighs. She wanted to wrap him like that. Good grief, she was jealous of cotton. She was a fool. All he had to do was look at her like that and her stupid legs ached to slip apart. Even more stupidly she was glad he hadn't given up on her. That it was her he was chasing, not all the bendable ballerinas currently rocking out on the grass. Yeah, there was her weakness—she wanted to be the one in front. She moved, quickly, taking a seat rather than leaning into him.

'We're not doing this.' She forced herself to say it. Tried to believe it. Glared harder at the dancers rehearsing their high kicks and tricks.

He took the seat next to her and put an arm around her shoulder. His fingers stroked down her bare skin with the casual ease of an intimate lover. She fought the urge to lean into the inviting breadth of his chest.

'Maybe if we got to know each other a little better, we'd discover all these things we didn't like about each other and our lust would die a quick death,' he drawled.

'You've told me all your angst already,' she answered, keeping her attention firmly on the girls on the grass. And it hadn't worked. The likelihood of her lust for him dying was as remote as the Silver Knights coming bottom of the table this season. For him, however, it was totally probable. Men didn't like home-wreckers, not even men who liked women fast and loose. And in truth men only wanted the fast women for a few quick thrills. She frowned. What they needed to do was steer the conversation away from the personal. She had to talk to him as politely as she did all the other guys. There didn't need to be an undercurrent of tension, of suggestion, in every word they swapped. She could normalise their interaction and thus neutralise the pull between them. Right?

'You don't like them, do you? The dancers.' He smashed through her thoughts, the teasing note gone from his voice.

'Why? You don't like other women stealing your limelight? You want to be the only babe on the block?'

Any idea of going polite on him fled at that. He was so wrong.

'Isn't that why you like working here?' He pressed her more. 'Why you don't have any girlfriend flatmates?'

'Maybe it's that they don't like me.' She turned her head, trying to hide the hit of his words.

His grin sharpened. 'Why wouldn't they like you? Are you too much of a man's woman?'

She shook her head but knew some thought it was true. In her home town her female friends had turned their backs and since she'd moved she hadn't actively sought to make new ones. All her effort had gone into her job. It was only recently she'd thought she needed to get out more. Ironically it was the dancers she'd been thinking of hanging out with.

'But you like being near those boys.' He scrutinised her. 'Being around successful people. Achievers. A girl who gravitates towards success.'

'To score myself a wealthy man?' Bitterness brewed and she scoffed. 'You couldn't be more wrong.'

'Really?'

'Yes.' She turned, riled enough to put him right on a few things. 'I've been surrounded by success my whole life, Seth. Hugely successful people. Way more successful than some ball player. You've got *no* idea. I was born after my super-intelligent sister and before my super-intelligent brother. There I am, Ms Totally Average, in the middle of two academic and sporting geniuses. So the last thing I want is to be overshadowed and overlooked even more.' She twisted. 'Do you know the only thing I've done that impressed my parents was meeting Cliff Richard? Seriously. Nothing I've actually achieved myself. My brother and sister are amazing—she's an academic, he's doing his PhD in engineering two years ahead of time while still playing semi-pro basketball. They were born that way—talking in complicated sentences in no time, winning every prize on offer since. I've never won a prize, Seth, not even for participation. And I've only got attention from my folks because of who I've met here. Not for anything I've actually done.'

Even the mess she'd made of her life all those months ago hadn't been enough to gain their undivided attention. At least, not initially. The full weight of disapproval and disappointment hadn't been expressed until their concern for the public perception of the family had been aired first. How it would impact on them. No wonder she'd been searching for the one thing they'd never given her—the feeling of being valued, special, wanted, supported—and finding it in the most wrong of places. But she refused to use her freakish family as her excuse; she was responsible for her own mistakes and she'd learned from them.

'They must be impressed with what you do here,' he said thoughtfully, his focus fully on her. 'It's a great job and you do it brilliantly.'

She really wanted to believe that they'd think that one day. There was still that part of her that wanted her parents' approval. She didn't know if that made her a fool or not. 'All I do is support other people. People far more successful than me.' The story of her life. 'I've been on the sidelines so long it's what I've become best at.'

'But you enjoy it.'

She paused, had to give him that. 'Yes, I do. As a job it's fantastic. But it shouldn't be all I am for my family, as well.'

'Lots of people couldn't do what you do,' he said. 'They couldn't handle all these egos and insecurities anywhere near as well. They couldn't handle working in the background.'

'If it's a talent, it's hardly a glam one.' Thoroughly under-appreciated.

'Don't underestimate it. It's hard to achieve big things alone,' he pointed out. 'Most people need a support crew.'

That made her pause. 'Did you have one?' Because he'd achieved far more than most people ever did. Then she remembered. 'Oh, no, your girl dumped you.'

He confirmed it with a small grin.

'What about your mum?'

His grin went rueful. 'No matter how many millions I make, I don't think she'll ever fully forgive me for quitting med school.'

'What about your dad?'

'He didn't give a damn.' His grin disappeared altogether. 'Maybe it would have been nice to have the kind of support you give those players.'

She tried to ignore the sweet feeling streaming from her chest to her limbs because she wasn't sure he'd ever needed anything from anyone. 'Maybe the lack of support is what drove you to succeed to the extent you have.'

She felt him draw breath but he answered lightly enough. 'Who knows?'

'Is that why you help these boys?' she asked. 'You give them the support you didn't have?'

He considered it. 'Not so much support as the skills to take charge of their own destiny. To fight a fight that's actually worth it. Some of those boys have had it a lot worse than I ever did. But I found sport gave me self-discipline, confidence and strength. It's okay to get angry, not okay to let that anger screw up your life. It works that way for lots of kids on the brink of losing it.'

He'd been on the brink? 'But you chose *boxing*?'

He chuckled. 'You don't like that? Don't tell me it's too violent for you, the rugby PR princess?' His shoulders shook. 'I knew we could find something to put you off if we talked for long enough.'

'I'm sure I can think of some other things not to like about you, as well,' she said tartly. But she was so curious about it. 'I thought you were too busy to make it to sports practice?'

'I was. But you can beat a boxing bag any time of day and then I found an old guy in a boxing hall who'd coach me at crazy hours.'

'Why did he agree to do that?'

'Because I was angry and he knew that would help me succeed. He was right.'

'Why were you angry?'

'Why is anyone angry?' he countered cryptically, leaning closer. They were sitting in the country's largest stadium, but the situation was unbearably intimate. 'But what about you—what is there not to like about you?'

There was only one answer to that. 'I want too much.'

'You reckon you're greedy?' His voice rose. 'Never.'

'I am.' Emotionally she couldn't get greedier. She wanted all the attention she'd missed out on.

'If you were greedy, we'd be having sex this second,' he muttered. 'Instead you're holding me at arm's length even though we both still want it. So why?' He speared her with that total intensity. 'You got an evil ex in your wardrobe, too?'

She blinked. Here it was, her chance to put him off. It would be so easy, because she didn't *have* the evil ex, she *was* the evil ex.

*I had an affair with a married man. I was the other woman. I tried to wreck someone else's happy home.*

Her excuses—the missing facts—screamed to be heard, too, but she blocked them. It was a sordid tale of utter stupidity. She'd been second best. She'd always been second best. Or worse.

And hadn't her own actions simply proved that was all she deserved to be? Because she wasn't smart. She wasn't a success anywhere near the league of her siblings. She wasn't worthy of the same amount of attention. She'd never got those moments of triumph; the celebratory dinners had never been in her honour.

Her evil-ex story would send him running for the hills. Turn the warmth in his gaze to disapproval because the double standard definitely still existed. Maybe she should just have another quick good time with him. Maybe that was all she was good for. But rebellion against that stereotype burned. Why couldn't she have a damn good time *and* the happy ever after? She wanted it all. But the guy to have that with wasn't lifelong-single-man Seth.

'You're not going to tell me, are you?' He finally filled the silence.

She didn't want to. Not here, not sitting in the late-summer sun under a sky as vividly blue as his eyes. It was another moment of fantasy and she didn't want to burst the bubble. Even though she knew she should sever the attraction between them, she just couldn't. 'I was young and naïve. Let's leave it at that.'

His hand cupped her jaw. 'I'll only leave it for another time.'

At that slight contact she melted closer. Excruciatingly aware of his body, she could almost feel his blood beating against her own. She drew a deep breath, trying to cool the inferno inside, but all it did was burn hotter. As if he could hear her thoughts, her secret wishes, his gaze travelled from her eyes to her mouth. She put her palm on his chest. Pleasure pierced from that lightest of touches. The heat and hard slam of his vitality were addictive. The scent of dawning summer intoxicated her.

He was irresistible. She leaned forward. She lifted her chin. She pressed her parted lips to his. She flicked his mouth with her tongue.

*She* did it. *She* wanted it. Oh, *how* she wanted it.

His response came instantly—but not the one she wanted. His head lifted—away—and in the next second he'd stood and moved to the railing. Well out of reach.

'You're punishing me for saying no before?' she asked, confused, then hurt, then annoyed.

'No, I'm proving restraint.'

'I didn't ask you to.'

'Maybe it's for me. Maybe I don't like the way this feels slightly out of control.'

Her heart thundered.

'That's some of what bothers you, too, isn't it?' he said softly, looking over his shoulder at her. 'That it's strong.'

She was his then, if only he knew it. But he was too far away to feel her head-to-toe tremble. And if he saw it, he gave no sign.

'I'm giving you one last chance to be certain that you want this,' he said. 'Because when we end up in bed again, it's going to be for a while. You need to be prepared for that.'

'No.' She shook her head. 'I won't agree.'

'You will.'

'I told you I don't want a fling.' She wanted it to be over. She wanted this wild flood to leave her so she was free to find someone ordinary. Someone who could care for her—just her—the way she ached to be cared for. Not this gorgeous over-achiever who could have every woman he wanted and would. Millions of them.

He lifted his chin, standing staunch.

'We can have one more night but that's it.' She would give herself that much. One more night to see it out.

'Not enough.'

Her heart stalled. 'I'm not going to change my mind.'

He walked up the steps towards the nearest stand exit and she wasn't sure if he meant her to hear him or not.

'You already have.'

# CHAPTER EIGHT

He was right, of course. Lena stood in the small conference room, ridiculously self-conscious in front of the youths. Tension sawed through her nerves and the unseasonably muggy weather shredded her concentration. She tried not to look at the man leaning against the back wall. Just the thought of him had kept her awake all night. And in the few minutes when she had snatched some sleep, he'd haunted her dreams. Oh, *how* he'd haunted them.

As soon as she was done she fled back upstairs and put some music on, thumped her keyboard as she worked to get her inbox emptier. Even so, she heard the playful shouts and calls from the kids now out on the field. Then both the music playing and the boys' noise were drowned by a drumming from overhead.

She ran to the viewing window. Hail. In late summer. Marble-sized balls of ice pitting the ground. Christchurch was famed for going through four seasons in one day, but this was just ridiculous.

The boys and Andrew were running off the pitch. But not Seth. He walked behind them, unfazed by the malevolence of the sudden storm, his tee shirt sodden in one second. It clung. He didn't hide his face from the ferocity of the hailstones; instead—as if he had some sixth sense—he looked up, searching.

She knew he saw her at the window because he stopped still. Despite the distance it was as if he could see into her soul. And it was burning hot for him. She put both her hands on the glass as if it could cool her. But there was only one thing that could douse her inferno.

Seth ran up the stairs and sprinted along the stadium's corridors. He knew he could have convinced her last night but he wanted absolute surrender. Now he knew he had it, but strangely his imminent victory didn't please him. Instead he felt unsettled. She'd opened up a little last night but not a lot. It only made him more curious. He wanted to know everything. And, damn it, his head was so messed he couldn't find her in this rabbit warren now.

Finally he got there. She stood exactly as he'd seen her from the pitch. A slim figure at the window in a navy dress with her hair sleek. Motionless, she gazed out at the mad weather. She couldn't have heard his footsteps over the din of the ice dump. He walked up behind her but kept an inch of space between them, not wanting to get her beautiful outfit all wet. But he reached out and placed his hands over hers, pressed them ever so slightly harder on the glass.

She didn't even flinch—she was that tense already, her muscles couldn't tighten more. So she had sensed him.

'Where are the boys?' Despite the hail hammering the steel roof, he heard her quiet whisper.

'With Andrew. Going to watch a DVD.'

'Shouldn't you be with them?'

'In a minute.'

He took half that minute to catch his breath. His chest ached as if he'd been working out for hours. But he hadn't; they'd hardly started. Which was how he felt about him and Lena.

'It's a big storm out there,' she murmured.

'Bigger one in here.'

She trembled—some emotion shivered through her from top to toe. Then he felt her force it to stop, tension locking her body still. He couldn't help himself, pressed a kiss to the juncture of her neck and shoulder.

'Not here.' Her whisper was a plea. A revelation of torment.

He felt another convulsion of her hands beneath his and realised that the resistance emanating from her wasn't against him, but herself. She was holding herself back.

He breathed deeper to contain the fierce reaction within himself. The things he wanted to do *now*—to press forward and pin her in place, to slide his hands beneath her dress, to get within her warmth as deeply and as quickly as possible. But as much as he wanted to, he wasn't going to drag her off for some two-second quickie in a cleaning cupboard. Not here, not now. They both had jobs to do. They both had to concentrate. And he'd meant what he'd said. He wanted more than one night. He wanted more than the frisky play they'd had the other day.

He wanted time. But that time wasn't now.

'Have dinner with me,' he said, unable to release her yet.

This time the small ripple within her was amusement. 'Is that what you call it?'

He'd heard her talk to the players, to the boys. He'd seen her do her stadium thing several times. He'd sparred with her, he'd had awesome sex with her. And her beauty, her knowledge, her enthusiasm and her professionalism all impressed him. But it was the laugh that felled him. Every time.

But he really meant for them to eat tonight, to converse. Because the snatches of flirt talk they'd shared so far weren't enough.

'I'll wait for you after work.' He forced himself to peel his hands off hers and stepped back. Beneath his ribs he still ached; he didn't stop to analyse why. All that mattered was seeing her and securing something more.

Lena bent her head, resting her forehead on the glass; it didn't ease her fever. She turned, pressing her spine against the pane. He was already at the end of the corridor, determinedly walking away and saving her from committing the cardinal workplace sin of having sex on-site. Because if he'd stayed a second longer, she'd have been begging him to. She couldn't fight it any more.

He was waiting for her outside her office at home time. They walked down to his car and he drove them straight into town.

'I am starving,' he said, pulling into a park that looked three metres too small for his car.

'We're really going out?' Lena released the breath from her bursting lungs. She'd been expecting the screech of car metal pranging but the guy seemed to know exactly how close to the edge he could go.

'What did you think I meant by "have dinner with me"?' His eyes twinkled as he waited for her on the footpath and then walked along with her.

'You know your track record speaks for itself.'

He just smiled. 'Are you okay with Japanese?' He opened a door with a flourish.

'Sure.' She breathed deeply as she walked into the exquisite interior. She'd never been there before, but she'd heard of it. It wasn't a restaurant, but a gastronomic mecca for those with overloaded wallets. Even the tiniest piece of sushi was rumoured to have a double-figured price tag.

The table was already booked, one at the back with the best view out of the window and the most privacy. His planning was nice, not that she'd read anything into it. He wined and dined the city's most beautiful. They would expect to come to an exclusive eatery like this. It wasn't that he was doing anything special just for her. But she would still enjoy it.

Despite the conspicuous lack of prices on the menu, Seth had no hesitation in ordering what seemed like a million dishes. They came out, one after the other, and Lena had to admit she could see why the place was famous.

'Fresh enough for you?' he teased as she tucked in.

'So fresh it's almost still swimming.' She giggled, snaffling another divine piece of sashimi. She sat back to savour it—both the food and the company. 'How's it going with the boys?' she asked him. 'Do you think it's helping?'

She listened as he talked through the highs and lows of the week so far. Asked him about previous ones. It turned out he was still in contact with several of his old 'graduates'. He'd even employed a couple of them. Another couple had actually gone to university. She suspected he was financially supporting them through it, but he didn't admit to that.

Both the food and the minutes disappeared as they talked. The conversation meandered easily, their laughter light and frequent. In part she was more relaxed than she'd ever been with him. In another part of her, the tension was only winding tighter. Inexorably its insistence grew—the pressure building, becoming louder and louder until it was suddenly the only thing she could hear. She looked at him, falling silent as she recognised the same tension banked in his eyes. It was that appetite that needed to be sated now.

'You're ready?' He broke the stillness with one of his multi-meaning questions.

'Yes.'

As they wound their way towards the exit, a light, delighted voice called, 'Seth!'

Another diner walked over to where she and Seth had stopped near the door.

'Hi, Rachel,' he greeted her with a broad smile, an arm around the waist and a kiss on the cheek.

Lena smiled through the introductions, listened to them briefly chat about people and places she didn't know. She tried not to stare at the woman, but did anyway. Thoughts tumbled and tormented. Seth was smiling and chatting to Rachel the same as he'd smiled and chatted with the dancers last night—all suave and charming. Only, Rachel was watching him attentively, was more familiar with him, as if she'd been the recipient of other intimacies. One of those willowy types with expensive clothes, she was all class. Not just beautiful, but smart, too. Refined.

Lena knew it was only a matter of time. She knew what to expect. Seth was with no one woman for long and it was better to be prepared—then it wouldn't hurt, right? She breathed out to ease the twisting knots in her stomach. Another tension entwined with the one that had been driving her. But hadn't she planned to be with him on her terms? Maybe she should set her terms out clearly. If she was going to be with a sophisticated playboy, then she needed to be sophisticated herself.

She smiled as Seth said goodbye to beautiful Rachel, smiled as the blonde insisted he call her sometime, and maintained that sophisticated smile as she bit the inside of her lip and refused to mention the woman once they were alone.

They didn't discuss anything as Seth drove to her apartment. Nor did they say anything as he accompanied her in, his hand tightly clasping hers. It was only once the door was shut and locked with them inside that one of them broke the silence.

It was Seth. He framed her face, lifting it to his. 'Lena.'

He kissed her with the kind of intensity that overwhelmed her. So good. His touch made her feel so exquisitely good.

Somehow they were in her bedroom already, somehow they were naked already, somehow she was feeling more than she meant to—not just physical excitement. And that could not be good.

She closed her eyes, that other tension sharpening. Her surging emotions made her vulnerable and her rearguard defence snapped to attention. She might have agreed to his more-than-once insistence, but she was determined to guide the path they were taking. She'd be sophisticated; *she'd* manage how this played out.

'This is just sex,' she said firmly. 'Nothing else. Not even a fling or anything, okay? We're just fixing the need. It's just a series of one-night stands.'

She could feel his smile as he kissed her shoulder. 'You're still trying to limit this?'

'It's not like you want anything more, either. And it's—' she hesitated for a second and then quickly said it '—not exclusive.'

He went very still. 'What did you just say?'

'You heard.'

He still didn't move and she swallowed, trying to moisten her sandpaper throat before repeating herself. 'Not exclusive.'

He looked up, his hot eyes stripped of humour—furious. He moved quickly, rising to straddle her, his hands on either side of her head.

'You're a very attractive man and I'd rather not be lied to.' She defended her position in a rush. Suddenly incensed because she knew it was inevitable anyway. She'd seen how that woman had looked at him. He was a temptation to any woman. 'I have no claim on you.'

'No, you understand this,' he said, leaning closer over her, utterly using his size to assert his dominance. 'I don't want to be lied to, either. I might not offer commitment, but

I'm all for exclusivity. No lies, no betrayal. No one else until this is over.'

She swallowed, suddenly burning with all kinds of emotion.

'I can't believe you think so little of me—like I'd do that?' He pushed down on the mattress, making her bounce the once. 'What's worse is that you think so little of yourself, because you'd actually put up with that.'

She was so livid she went light-headed. 'You kissed me as a total stranger and we had sex after a bare ten minutes of talking,' she snarled.

'And we both know that's not something you usually do, so why can't it be something I don't usually do, too?'

She stared up at him, furiously waiting for him to answer that one all by himself.

'Okay, maybe I've not been as celibate as you in recent months,' he growled. 'But I want you and no one but you and I respect both of us enough to keep it that way until those feelings change. I'm not going to lie to you and I sure as *hell* expect the same from you. No other women, no other men. Agreed?'

'Fine,' she snapped back.

Seth was rock hard and overwhelmed by a primitive urge to conquer her completely. So that when she wanted, when she begged, it would be only him she begged for. *Never* any other man. He hated the idea of her with someone else. *Never* had he felt possessiveness bite so deep. Damn it, he wanted to know what the hell was going on in her head.

He lunged forward, throwing the weight of his body over hers so she couldn't escape. He grabbed her wrists, lifting them high above her head so her breasts were thrust up and she was back at his mercy. He looked down at her rich, vulnerable curves and took a second to debate just how he was going to make her pay.

He felt it ripple in her body. Her response rising to equal his. Her legs parted; he felt her curl one around his hips, trapping him as much as he'd trapped her.

Oh, yes, while he imprisoned her with his hands and weight, she imprisoned him with her legs—and then her sex. She arched quickly, her legs clamping, sheathing him wholly and holding him tight. And then she moved—furiously milking him for the pleasure she wanted. Thirsty, hedonistic, wanton.

His challenge to answer, and heaven help him, he loved it.

The tone changed as the exquisite sensations neutralised anger and enhanced nothing but that sublime need. He told her exactly what he wanted and she purred right back at him— what she wanted, how she wanted, *now.* Their words slapped together as explicitly as their bodies were. Hot, rough, honest.

Her demands drove him harder, further inside her silken web. Fast, breathless, beautiful. Until finally Seth saw her down and made her scream as he savagely poured his whole strength into her—the woman who was as wild, as proud and as playful as he.

# CHAPTER NINE

When Lena woke she couldn't bear to turn and face Seth for a moment as she remembered all the things they'd said and done through the night. At his wicked insistence, she'd expressed every single one of her most secret, physical desires. Desires she'd never dared whisper aloud even to herself before. He'd met her need, matched it and made the reality so much better than fantasy. And now? Now there were even more fantasies.

But she was older, wiser, stronger than the naïve girl she'd been eighteen months ago. She now knew sex didn't equal love. And having sex wouldn't make someone fall in love with you. It didn't work that way. Seth was an extremely generous, adventurous lover but his determination to fulfil her every sensual desire meant nothing more. And while her non-exclusive offer might have been a mistake, he was still a sophisticate. He was not the let's-get-married long-term kind of guy. She had to hold on to that. She had to protect her heart. But, oh, she couldn't say no to this fling now.

For the next few days Seth steered clear of her as much as he could at the stadium. But the second that Andrew had loaded the boys back into the van and driven them off to their homes, he was in his car, impatiently waiting for her to join him. He took her out to dinner—traded stories, jokes, and tried to break through the barriers that he knew were still there.

He might be back in her bed but it wasn't enough. An uneasy hunger remained. He decided the best way to deal with it was to be with her the entire weekend—the best way of getting to know her more, the best way to get rid of the desire that still crunched his bones at the mere thought of her. So on Friday night he took her to his apartment. The big space he liked to keep to himself. But this was necessary.

He scooped up the pile of guff that had been posted through the slot in the door over the past few days and that now blocked their access to the stairs leading to his loft. He'd only raced in each day to grab clean clothes and then headed to the stadium, gone to her house each night. But bringing her here now made him feel as if he could control the duration—he figured she couldn't kick him out of his own apartment.

'You get the newspaper delivered?' She chuckled, watching him balance the fat rolls of newsprint and the advertising circulars and lead the way upstairs. 'You don't read it online?'

'You can't do the crossword online,' he answered with mock horror. 'Not the same.'

The husky note in her laugh deepened.

Stupidly happy, he got to the top floor and dumped the armload of papers and circulars straight in the bin by his worktable. He wasn't going to have the time to go near any crossword in the next few hours.

'Wait, there's a letter tucked in with that.' She reached down past him and pulled out the envelope.

Seth frowned. Most of his mail came electronically and what didn't went to his business address. He glanced at the writing. Damn. He took it from her, trying to keep casual.

It wasn't the first, but he'd hoped the woman would have got the message. Because he'd never opened her past notes and he wasn't going to now.

Lena was watching him. He realised he'd been quiet too long.

'I get a lot of begging letters.' He dismissed it, tossed the thing back in the bin. And that was exactly what it would be. His father's wife wanting money. He saw Lena's gaze linger on it and he kicked the bin further under the table.

'So.' He turned his back on old history to take advantage of a far more enjoyable moment. 'Wanna see my bedroom?'

Her smile went wicked. 'What, you've got no flatmates to introduce me to?'

Of course he damn well didn't. Looking at him, she laughed. Because of course she damn well knew it.

He hauled her into his arms and marched to his bedroom. Planned to keep her with him until he was bored. Surely it wouldn't take that long? He'd always got bored by spending too much time with one girl before. Pretty quickly, too. But despite seeing her every day and night for the best part of a week already, he was so very far from bored. He set her on her feet, watched her turn to face him with her head high and her eyes gleaming. Definitely not bored, he was right back to spellbound.

'Lie down.' She stood proudly, seeming to size both the bed and him up.

He sent her a long look letting her know that whatever he did would be his decision, not her order. But he now understood that she had a real need to feel as if she was in charge of their affair. He just wished she'd trust him enough to tell him why. Then he might admit to her that he didn't think it was within either of their control any more. But she already had a condom in her hand, so he figured that conversation could wait a few minutes yet.

He let her ride him slow, smoothed down her back with the heels of his hands and watched her arch to meet his touch. He adored her lush enjoyment. She was fearless of their physical passion at least. She muttered his name again and again, her rhythm lifting. He cupped her breasts, coasted a caress down to her narrow waist, dying inside as she rocked and twisted. Oh, she knew how to squeeze and tease him. He couldn't think, couldn't resist a fierce thrust up, taking her hips in a tight grip and urging her faster and harder.

'Oh.' She complied with his guidance—so much faster and harder than he'd dreamed. 'Seth!'

He really needed to silence her because every time her husky voice sounded he was shoved another metre to the edge. But in a heartbeat and a hiss he was submerged in hot, wet flames of ecstasy. It was for ever before he realised that the long groan of delight was his.

As he blinked he felt her shaking. He pulled her close and breathed heartfelt thanks she'd come the second after he had. Only, in that actual second, he'd been too out of it to know and he didn't want to miss out on seeing and feeling her that way.

He flipped her over and spread her legs, sliding down and sucking so the sensations within her wouldn't stop. He reached up to cup her breasts again, palming her tightly budded nipples while he ate her hot, wet sweetness. He teased with his lips and tongue, couldn't get enough. He wanted it to go on and on—this tension that put her at his mercy.

She twisted, screaming his name, shuddering as she gave in. Her shoulders lifted, her hands clawing air, as he wrung her passion free. He loved her ability to slide from one orgasm to the next. He loved to see just how far he could push her. But he still couldn't seem to get as close as he wanted.

In the morning Lena pulled herself out of his bed and went in search of food. She found bread and toasted some. Seth wandered out and snagged a piece from her plate and refilled the toaster as he ate. Munching, she walked around the giant open-plan room. She liked his apartment. It was in the old industrial side of the inner city—a number of bars and boutique fashion shops had opened post-earthquake, fairy lights strung through the narrow lanes that had once been back entrances to big, dirty warehouses, art installations filled spaces between reconstruction. She knew he was responsible for much of the redevelopment. His personal space was very hip, very big and very sparse. Other than the sofa and a big table and some chairs, there wasn't other furniture. And while he did have the obligatory boy toys of stereo and computer, games console, there was one obvious gadget missing.

'No telly?' she asked as he fiddled with the coffee machine.

'Don't need one, never watch it.'

'What about sport?' She knew he was an enthusiast.

'Prefer to participate than spectate.' He winked.

'Oh, come on, what about the big games?'

'There's always a pub or mate's place.' He shrugged.

Somehow she doubted he went to either much. It was obvious from the table that he put in huge hours of work here—the walls were covered with plans, with notes written in a masculine scrawl all over them. In the far corner of the room a boxing bag hung and gloves were tossed on the floor. She turned her back on that. At one point along the wall a collection of books lay in a messy heap on the floor—clearly once a tower of serious-looking tomes that had been toppled. The only things on the walls were some building plans tacked up near the computer table. There were no clues to his past but perhaps the lack of photos and personal items was the biggest clue of all.

'Where does your mum live?' she couldn't resist asking as he poured the coffee thick and black.

'In sunny Nelson.'

'That where you grew up?'

He shook his head. 'She moved there a few years ago.'

'Does she work?'

He took a big sip of what had to be burning-hot coffee. 'Yeah.' He inhaled sharply. 'I can't stop her.'

'What does she do?'

'She's a cleaner,' he answered, carefully neutral.

Lena said nothing, and in less than three seconds he was answering her unasked question anyway.

'I hate it.' Gruff, low, rough. 'I paid off her mortgage but she refuses to take more money from me and cleaning is what she's always done. Dad left her with nothing and even before he left he just did jack all in his shed all day. She always worked a zillion jobs and as soon as I was old enough I worked, too, to help her out. But now she insists on working even though she doesn't have to.'

'Maybe she likes her independence,' said Lena, frankly full of admiration for the woman. No prizes for guessing where Seth had got his fighting spirit from, either. 'Not many people would actually enjoy a life with nothing to do but shop or do lunch anyway.'

He looked sceptical. 'You reckon?'

'Seriously,' Lena said, fully meaning it. 'Getting up for work gives you a kind of dignity. A purpose. *You* couldn't live a life of leisure, could you?'

He shook his head.

'So why think she would?'

'Because she's worked hard enough,' he said crossly. 'If

she wants to be busy, she could work for a charity or something. She doesn't have to be on her hands and knees.' His hands lifted in a frustrated movement. 'I've never been able to—'

She watched him sharply turn away. 'To what?'

'Give her what she needs.'

Lena was touched. And troubled. Because was that his responsibility? With every child and parent there were expectations—Lena well knew that. There were burdens, too—on both sides—but maybe they were greater for an only child and for a solo parent. She felt frustration within him, sensed the hurt there. She wrapped her arms around his waist from behind, giving him a cuddle more of companionship than carnal thrill. 'Maybe she doesn't want to burden you. She had an unhappy time with the divorce, right? Maybe she needs to feel like she can manage on her own now.' Lena could so relate to that. 'She's *your* mother, Seth. And you love nothing more than your independence.'

He slowly turned, his arms lifting to return her hug, and she felt his reluctant smile. 'I just want her to be happy.'

'Do you think she isn't?' she asked softly.

'No, she always says she's great.'

'Then maybe you should relax and let her do what she needs to do.' Lena snuggled into his tightening embrace. 'She's her own person, Seth. Like you. And no one can take on the total responsibility of another person's happiness. It's a balance, you know? Team effort.'

She felt him sigh and shake his head a fraction. 'Lena in sweetheart, supportive mode. No wonder all those boys want you to oil their chests.'

She rolled her eyes, refusing to take his light joke any more seriously than he intended.

They hung out on the sofa, with the coffee and toast and his iPad—surfing the news, checking out the social network sites. She had all day and all night to talk with him—about the team or any other sport, music, buildings, construction, food, travel tales, to laugh at random stories about stars behaving badly. There was no guilt, no pressure. And despite knowing she was going to regret it, she dived into the bliss headfirst.

She'd put one of his tee shirts on. Seth didn't mind. He probably should have warned her he was keeping her captive for the weekend, then she could have brought some clothes. Still, her not having them did have its benefits.

He caught her eyeing the punchbag swinging from a hook in the corner with disfavour.

'You really hate boxing?' He laughed as he watched her nose wrinkle.

'I like most sports, probably more than many people do. But boxing is just a step too far for me. It's not really a sport, is it?'

'Hmm.' He walked over to pick up his gloves. 'You've never got so angry you felt like hitting something?'

She frowned. 'I don't see how boxing can help with anger issues. Doesn't it just teach troubled kids how to hurt people?'

'No,' he said patiently. 'It teaches discipline, control and builds confidence.'

'So does yoga.'

He ran his palm down the punchbag and sighed. 'Okay, it's also a fantastic physical and mental release. One-to-one combat, the ultimate individual challenge. No team-mate to back you up, no one else to blame if you crash out. Just you against your opponent. So you have to learn self-reliance, self-discipline and have self-belief.' He held out the gloves. 'Dare you. You might find you like it.'

'I don't think so.'

'Go up against the bag, just once.'

She grimaced but wriggled the gloves on. They were too big but it didn't matter. She took aim and the frankly pathetic punch didn't make it swing even a millimetre.

She giggled. 'Nope, not doing it for me.'

He moved in behind her, showed her the way to move her arm. 'Focus. Visualise. Go for it.'

He stood back again and watched her second effort— even worse. 'Okay.' He changed tack. 'Turn around and try to hit me.'

She turned but didn't follow through. 'Never in a million years.'

'Go on, I'm sure I'll have taken worse.'

Her green eyes widened. 'I'm not going to hurt you.'

'Well, no,' he drawled. 'I'm not going to let you do that.'

Her stance snapped straighter as she sparked. 'You're not going to let me?'

Oh, he'd tweaked her nerve. Good. 'Try to hit my hands.' He waggled his palms in front of her.

Her searing gaze narrowed.

'One to one, you see,' he teased. 'Just you and your opponent.'

She struck out. Missed him, of course, because he was fast. It was one of his strengths.

'That the best you got?' he taunted.

'Oh, don't start with the wind-me-up-to-get-me-going rubbish.'

'Why not?' he taunted. 'It's always worked before.'

She was half laughing but half-serious, too. So was he.

'Come on.' He moved closer. 'Come and get me.'

She jabbed a couple more times. He let her connect to his chest once.

That made her frown thunderous. 'Don't go easy on me.'

'Okay, then try harder.'

She moved fast on him then, a series of wild-thrown

punches. Getting better. Breathing hard, her cheeks flushed, she kept at it, trying to get him good. As she'd asked, he didn't make it easy for her. But he praised when she hit him square, issued instructions to help her. Her small fists smacked loudly on his palms, not doing damage, but a nice workout for her. He knew it. Smugness made him slow for a second—so did the fact that her tee-shirt-and-knicker combo was turning him on. And at that exact moment, the wench kicked him.

'Ow.' He muffled his curse as he rubbed his shin. 'What the hell was that? Kicking isn't in the rules.'

'There are *rules* in boxing?' She shrieked with laughter and girly-danced around him—doing a gleeful Rocky impersonation with her hands in the air. 'I thought it was just a free-for-all. And you know I just made you drop your guard.'

'It's about a whole lot more than winning, you know.' He snatched the gloves off her and pulled her close.

'Rubbish,' she challenged him right back. 'All anyone wants is to win.'

The afternoon went far too fast. They lunched lazily at a café down the street, wandered through the gallery, then returned to his apartment for an afternoon 'nap'. Lena did almost doze for a while, dreamily thinking about their little sparring round. He'd been right; she'd enjoyed it more than she'd thought she would. Mainly because she thought she understood him more—that his determined self-reliance had been built from his turbulent teen years. His choice of an individual competitive sport over a team one showed his need to be his own boss. Just like his business dealings now. He was determinedly independent. Took all responsibility on his shoulders. Him against the world—him alone. No permanent business partner, no permanent life partner. It made her heart ache.

By the early evening they were snacking in the kitchen. Lena was in another of his tee shirts and wondering if she ought to be sensible and go home.

'I know why you keep looking at your watch,' he said suddenly. 'The game tonight. The Knights are playing in Wellington and you want to watch it.'

Actually she'd forgotten all about the game. 'It's okay,' she said. 'I know they'll win.'

'Come on.' He stood. 'I know a great place where we can see it in style.'

'Really?' Well, if he was up for it she definitely was. While it was part of her job to be interested, in truth she genuinely loved it. She thought her passion for the game was what had got her the job in the first place. 'I can't wear this, though.' She gestured to her man-tee-and-knickers combo. 'I'll get back into my dress.'

'No, actually that shirt'll be perfect. I'll find you some jeans.'

She stared. As if she were going to fit his jeans, as if she would wear them out in *public*. Amazed, she watched as he actually went to the trouble of punching an extra hole in one of his belts with a hammer and nail so she could wear it to hold up the jeans he'd tossed at her. With her kitten-heeled mules it was so not the look. 'I can't go out like this.'

'Sure you can, you'll fit right in.'

Dubiously she checked him out; he was wearing ultra-casual, too, but then he could wear anything and look amazing.

'Come on.' He laughed. 'Kick-off in ten—you don't want to miss the pre-game analysis, do you?'

They walked more in the direction of the urban badlands than the chic area where the restaurants were. Yeah, it was a graffiti-covered, falling-down-fences kind of alley that he led her down.

'You bring all your girls here?' She looked at the poorly lit bar and the collection of biker-gang vehicles lined up in front of it.

'This place hasn't been designated as urban cool yet but it's only a matter of time,' he joked lightly, but then sent her a concerned look. 'Don't worry, you're safe with me.'

She wasn't afraid, she was amused. She mock jabbed the air in front of her with a quick one-two punch. 'Don't need you to protect me, I got my moves.'

'Uh-huh, you're a real karate queen.' For once he didn't hold the door and wait for her to go first; this time he squared up and walked in ahead of her as if he were the beefy security guard checking out the scene for the in-disguise star who'd broken out to have her dangerous night on the wrong side of town.

'What's so funny?' he asked as he caught her grin.

She shook her head, not going to reveal the ridiculous-ness of her thoughts.

The place was miles from glam, but bolted to the wall was the biggest screen she'd ever seen. On the opposite wall there was another. 'Oh.' She nodded. 'Hidden treasure.'

'Don't think they do champagne, though.' He winked.

No, clearly the focus here was beer, spirits and sport.

'I'm happy with a shandy,' she said, referring to a lager-and-lemonade mix.

'And my credibility is killed.' He kept her close with his hand on hers while he ordered. They carried the drinks to a high table near the back corner. The stools were wooden but she preferred hard and clean to soft and sticky spilt-brew covered anyway. The crowd was growing, kick-off was in five.

Lena took a sip and opened one of the packets of peanuts he'd grabbed, her eyes glued to the screen, listening to the commentators appraising each side's starting line-up.

Seth found himself watching her just as much as the action on the big screen. It was hilarious. He soon learned he could tell how well the Knights were playing by the narrowness of her eyes. Her slight frowns lightened and deepened accordingly. Her cheers when they scored were fantastic and the smile she turned towards him sublime.

Then there was the running commentary. It started as just the movement of her lips, as if she was uttering some incantation beneath her breath. But as the on-screen action intensified, her volume upped.

'Oh, what are you doing?' she called, her frown growing. 'Get in there. Get the ball!'

He wondered if she expected them to answer. He swigged from his bottle to hide his smile.

'Come on.' She nearly leapt from her stool. *'Ruck!'*

Seth snorted and nearly choked on his beer. Coughing loudly, he put his bottle down on the table with a loud bang.

She turned to him with a quelling look, waiting for him to recover. 'You thought I said something else, didn't you?' she said oh-so primly. 'You think I'd use that kind of language?'

He held her gaze, barely suppressing his laughter. 'Well, I do recall you telling me to "ruck" you the other night… or maybe I misheard and it was something else you said.' Wickedly amused, he watched her blush bloom. 'Actually it wasn't what you said that was so funny just now.'

'No?' She might still sound cucumber cool, but her cheeks were cherry coloured.

'Lena,' he drawled, totally patronisingly, as if she were some child he had to speak extra slow for. 'I know the screen's big, but it's still a telly. They. Can't. Hear. You.'

She picked up the bag of peanuts and started pelting him, laughing when he ducked to try and catch them in his mouth. Ten seconds later she tossed the bag down, mock miffed when he actually got one.

'You just can't handle the fact I know more about this game than you do.' She sniffed.

'You do know more about it than most.' He'd give her that. And he was enjoying her commentary an insane amount. So, he'd noticed, were some of the other men sitting nearby.

'I work for a rugby club, so I guess I should,' she said smugly.

'Imagine you on the sideline when you have kids,' he teased. 'The poor things, you'll be yelling at them left and right.'

'I'm not going to be a pushy parent.'

'So you say now.'

'No, really I'm not,' she said, more vehemently than when she'd been yelling at the players on-screen. 'They can do whatever, be whatever. They don't have to make Olympic-gold standard. They can just be and I'll love them for it.'

Silenced for a moment, Seth looked at her—watched her mouth firm as she pulled that burst of emotion back in. 'Was it really that bad?' he asked bluntly.

Her sideways look sliced. 'You're a winner, Seth. You don't know what it's like for us mortals.'

'No?'

'No.' She shook her head with a hurt little laugh. 'You can't even imagine.'

He tried a grin. She didn't grin back.

Instead she leaned forward, her expression intense. 'You should have seen the celebrations. My parents really know how to throw a party for those moments of triumph. But it had to be a win. My siblings got all the winner genes. I got the recessive failure ones. Someone had to, I guess.' She spluttered a little smile. 'But there was no lowering the bar for the less-able athlete. It was high set and I never cleared it.' She shook her head. 'My mum and dad are both lawyers. The corporate-shark kind. They met at uni—were both on the rep tennis team. They're achievers and they expected us to achieve. The household was never happier than when success was on the table. Winners got parties, got prestige. And they all worked for it, they *really* worked. But I worked, too. I tried. But trying wasn't enough. You couldn't just try your best. You had to *be* the best.' She paused. He saw her swallow and take a breath.

'I love my brother and sister and I'm proud of them but I'm envious, too. How could I ever compete? I couldn't. I know it wasn't intentional, but I got sidelined. It's why I'm good on the sidelines now—it became my niche. But it was so busy—every school holiday we'd be at some national sports meet or maths challenge or something. They'd talk strategy and training over dinner. So much *time* went into them. All the time.'

'What did you do while your parents focused on them?'

'If the support act wasn't needed I watched the rugby.' She laughed but it was a sad laugh. 'I liked it. And you know in this country there's always a game on.'

'Lena,' he tried to reassure her, 'not everyone can win every time.'

'Oh, they can. Case in point.' She nodded to the screen, where the Knights had just scored a try. 'And just as there are some who always win, there are others who never do.'

'It's wrong to be that fixated on it. There's more to life.'

'Yeah, there is. And I look at the pressure they put on themselves and I think that's so crazy. But it's how our family works. It's how we're supposed to find happiness. I wanted to be successful in the way our family measures it.'

'You didn't rebel? You didn't go off the deep end and try to get attention some other way?' He'd pushed it that way for a while after the divorce. Until he'd realised the only person he was hurting was himself.

She was silent for a while. 'I did screw up over something,' she said quietly. '*Really* screwed up. Looking back, I guess it was attention related. In the end I told them because I needed them. I knew I'd stuffed up. Everyone knew I'd stuffed up. And I needed my parents to…support me.…' She'd whitened.

He was careful not to ask what it was, even though he was dying of curiosity. Because he was finally seeing how this was for her. And it clearly wasn't good. 'How'd they react?'

'The first question they asked was whether anyone else knew,' she whispered. 'They were most worried that others would know and judge. Like it was going to blow their prestige. Their first thought wasn't whether I was okay. It wasn't even to yell at me for being such a freaking fool. I'd have preferred it if they'd done that. It might have meant more.'

'Were you okay?' His heart rammed his rib cage, over and over, as he wondered about what it was she'd done. Trouble with the law seemed most likely—drunk driving or dabbling in drugs or something. Hell, he wanted to know. But he bit back from asking—just had to be patient and hope she'd tell him.

'Yeah.' She nodded. 'I left town. Started over.'

Silence. Seth waited but knew with each ticking moment that she wasn't going to tell him more. He breathed out the disappointment. And then made himself put on a little teasing smile. 'Well, what they think doesn't matter so much anyway, right?'

Her eyes widened and he saw how deep the sadness went. 'They're my *parents*.'

Yeah, she didn't see that one as a joke.

'What child doesn't want to please their parents?' she

asked in amazement. 'Right at the core, don't you want to know they love you and approve of you?' She stared at him for a moment. Then sighed. 'Actually you've probably never doubted that. You've achieved so much your parents can't be anything but super proud.'

She was wrong. And suddenly Seth wasn't seeing the lighter side, either. Because his success hadn't been enough for his father. Right from when he was a young kid Seth's academic ability had been commented on. As had his athleticism. But so what? His father hadn't stayed. His mother had still been unhappy. Both had wanted other—or more—kids. He hadn't been enough, done enough, for either of his parents. His experience was the antithesis of Lena's. He'd been the achiever. But he'd still failed on the attention front. On the ability to please or to make happy.

'It shouldn't matter so much,' he said firmly. 'You should be happy with your choices and your job. If your family can't see all you have to offer, if they can't celebrate your spirit, that's their loss.' He figured she should forget about them. It was better not to buy into all that. Better to be on your own. That was what worked for him.

'I know you're right. And I'm trying. I've got a job that plays to my strengths and that I love. Maybe one day they'll appreciate the success I have in it. Or maybe they won't. Even though I'm doing my thing, there's always that little part that wants it from them. Approval, attention, *anything.*'

Seth shifted uncomfortably on his stool.

'If I ever have kids I'm never going to let them doubt my belief in them or my love for them,' she said. 'No matter how bright or how sporty they may or may not be.'

He just nodded. She really did feel it—less loved by her parents because she wasn't as successful as her siblings. And he could see why. He didn't have siblings—well, none who counted—but it must have sucked to live in the shadow of their success. It must have sucked to feel alone within a family. He watched her lift her glass and take a man-sized gulp of her watered-down drink. He was sorry for bringing it up. He hadn't meant to dampen her spirits; originally he'd been out to make her laugh *more*.

He glanced up to the screen and caught the end of some stunning play. 'Hey, your young rookie just stopped that other guy getting a try.'

She glanced up in time for the replay. Her smile materialised instantly. Huge and warm. And that made him smile. He eased back and watched her watching the Knights cane the opposition.

Never had he considered bringing a woman to this shack before midnight. But sitting at the back of this dodgy old bar with her wearing his jeans and tee, drinking beer and shouting instructions at players who couldn't hear them, was one weird, wonderful joy.

Monday night Lena finished work early. Other than the usual training sessions, there was nothing on at the stadium until the end of the week. She hurried home and showered, her excitement sizzling—still on a high from the most fun-filled weekend of her life. He'd said he'd be round as soon as he'd finished work. She dressed, did her hair, couldn't wait to see him. But she did wait. Waited and waited.

She stared at her mobile, began waiting for the excuse. But it didn't land. Her phone remained silent and her blood congealed. So it had started—the breaking of plans and promises.

It was almost three hours before she finally slapped some spirit back into herself. What was she doing? She wasn't going to sit around waiting. Hadn't she wasted enough hours of her life waiting for a man who'd never followed through in the end? Who'd taken her 'anytime' availability for granted.

Just as Seth was starting to now.

This was a perfect reminder of what they were actually doing—*nothing* more than sex. The sweet security of a deepening bond she'd thought she'd felt in the weekend had been nothing but a façade. So much for thinking that she was starting to understand his loner lifestyle. In reality he was just another guy who'd never want his freedom hampered.

A night apart was just what she needed to get her defences back up. And if she could survive one night without him, she could survive two, then three, then four. She still had a grip on it—right? Her wayward heart.

But she was going to need some distraction to help her. A night out would be the answer. She was dressed up, why waste the look? She ignored the fact she hadn't been out in for ever, that she didn't have anyone to go out with. That she didn't even know where to go. But she'd just got to the end of her path when his car pulled up. He cut the engine and leaned across to open the passenger door. A stylish bunch of flowers on the seat made her more angry. Her favours and forgiveness could not be *bought*—she wasn't that naïve any more.

'I'm sorry, I got—'

'It's fine,' she lied.

There was a short, sharp silence.

'Have you eaten?' he asked.

'Of course. Did you expect me to wait? I didn't know what time you'd be here and I don't like sitting around hungry.' Oh, yes, she was ticked and happy for him to know it.

He drew a deep breath. 'Lena—'

'I can't stop, I'm going out.'

'It's a Monday night.'

'Monday is the new Friday, didn't you know? And I've got tomorrow off so it's even more of a party night for me.'

'Right,' he answered less calmly. 'You want me to party with you?'

'No.' She needed to reclaim her life and push him out of it. Seeing him every night wasn't going to work. She'd be swallowed up, turned into the beck-and-call support act—that he didn't want. And being the support act was never great—the audience was never that interested, barely paid attention, talked their way through the set.

The tragedy was that supporting was what she was best at. She was a pro at organising the tours and events for the real stars. For getting what they wanted when they wanted it. But she damn well wasn't going to do that for her lover. Not even her one-night-stand lover. She wanted to be the headline act in her own affair. Not be taken for granted as the person who provided the perks.

He regarded her steadily. 'You're angry with me.'

She didn't answer because her dominant emotion now was *hurt* and that was pathetic.

'I'm not a mind-reader, Lena,' he said. 'You said you don't play games, so level with me. What have I done wrong?'

She bent down to look at him direct through the car window. 'Don't bring me flowers for forgiveness. And if you're going to be late or not show, just let me know.'

'I'm sorry I'm later than you expected,' he said. 'I had a meeting that went on and there was some stuff that impacted from there. I have a ton to catch up on after my absence from the office last week.'

She heard the edge in his tone and felt a bitter victory at putting him in a bad mood, too.

'Not a lot of point in my telling you the truth if you choose not to believe me,' he said even more sharply.

'You could have sent a message.'

'So I could, if I hadn't been in a dead spot.'

They were in the second largest city in New Zealand. There weren't cell-phone dead zones in this town.

His eyes narrowed. 'You still don't believe me? You're almost as untrusting as I am—now, why is that?' He leaned across to see her face. 'Did someone really hurt you?'

She stood upright, breaking eye contact. 'I hurt myself.'

He waited for her to say more.

She didn't.

Eventually he growled, 'Can I give you a lift to wherever you're going?'

'No, thanks.'

'Fine.' He didn't fight her. 'Then I'll see you later.'

She walked, head high, refusing to watch him depart. But she was so pathetic she listened for the engine long after it was gone.

She didn't go to a bar or club or even a movie. She went to the twenty-four-hour supermarket and picked up an extremely nasty crime novel. She needed the certainty of seeing the bad guy get it.

# CHAPTER TEN

SETH prowled round his apartment. Pissed off because he was tired and stressed and couldn't sleep. So he'd been late—there were worse things to be. And how hideous of him to buy her flowers? Hell, he didn't need the drama. It was a good thing he had to fly out first thing tomorrow. Some space would be good. He'd been seeing too much of her anyway, right? Was getting bored already, right?

Hell, no.

He paced along the windows, looking out at the quiet city. Monday—not exactly the night for raves. Where would she have gone? Who would she have met up with? He didn't think she had that many friends. And that was weird because Lena was a team player if ever he'd met one. She thrived on the group atmosphere at the stadium. So why didn't she have flatmates? Why did she spend her whole life working? Why was she so determined to stay single? He wanted to know who had burned her. And how. And why she refused to open up to him on that.

His mood worsened. Damn it, he'd been looking forward to seeing her. He *had* been getting to know her more and the more he had, the more he wanted to. Truthfully he didn't want to go away tomorrow. He'd avoided Auckland for a long time, concentrating on building his portfolio in Christchurch and Wellington instead. But this was too good an opportunity to pass up and he was a man, not a wimpy boy. But still, he wished Lena were here now to distract him—because memories were lingering, feeding his malcontent. Stupid to let things that had happened so long ago still bother him this much.

He took another turn around his apartment. Big and empty and boring. He wished she were on the sofa and laughing about something stupid as she had last night. He wished he could take her in the plane with him tomorrow and go somewhere else altogether—away from the pressure.

Damn. That wasn't a bad idea.


Someone banged on Lena's door at a hideously early hour of the morning. She opened it and her vulnerable heart showered happy vibes around her body, dispelling her lingering grump from the night before.

'Come with me today,' he said straight off, wearing a sensational suit and an irresistible smile.

Lena wrinkled her nose and made a last stand for independence. 'I was planning to do some shopping.' She didn't know what for.

'You can do that any time. Come for a ride. I want to spend the day with you. Please.'

He got her just like that—with a line that struck at her weakest spot. Because she wanted to be wanted. She wanted him to want to be with her as much as she wanted to be with him.

'Okay.' Too easy, but she didn't care. She'd missed him. 'I need ten minutes.'

'Sure.' He glanced at the mess that was her hair. 'Late night?'

She nodded. She'd read the crime story cover to cover, hadn't switched out the light 'til after 4:00 a.m.

He drove. She didn't pay attention to the direction, too

happy to be in his company. But her curiosity leapt when he pulled into one of the side entrances of the airport.

'Where are we going?'

'That's our ride.' He pointed as he pulled into a private car park.

She looked at the gleaming machine waiting on the tarmac. 'You don't think I'm getting in that, do you?'

'Why wouldn't you?' he asked. 'You a nervous flier?'

'Don't you know it's always the rich jerks who think they're capable of anything who kill themselves in their private planes?' She had no plan to become one of those statistics. 'I'll happily go commercial, but I'm not getting into that flying coffin.'

He walked towards the plane, not bothering to hide his amusement. 'Lena, this is a jet. This doesn't fly as low as those little things that go into mountains.'

'Big planes go into mountains, too. Much bigger. Do you fly it?'

'You don't trust me to?'

'Of course not,' she said hotly. 'You're a glorified salesman. I'm not going up there with a part-time pilot who's got more confidence than sense.'

'So you're saying no? You think you're so good at that,' he jeered.

She glared but he grinned—calm, at ease—while she grew both hotter and colder. Because, as tempted as she was, she *wasn't* going to go up there, with him at the controls. But time pulled that trick again—it liked to bend when she looked at him. Only, he broke the moment and turned away. Belatedly she heard footsteps. She'd been too dazzled by his beautiful eyes to even blink.

'Meet Mike.' Seth put his hand on her waist and drew her forward.

Beneath her dress her skin sizzled. So much for thinking

a night apart from him would begin to break her addiction. Her need seemed worse now.

'Hello.' Habit helped her smile and hold out her hand to the man who'd strolled out of the hangar.

'Mike's a *full-time* pilot,' Seth stressed. 'And he'll be flying us today.'

'Oh.' Surprised, Lena looked harder at Mike. 'Really?'

Mike smiled. 'I'm just doing the final checks,' he said to Seth. 'Take-off in five okay for you?'

'Great.' Seth nodded. 'You want to freshen up before we go?' He turned back to her. 'There are facilities in the hangar.'

'No, thanks,' she murmured, taking in the beautiful sleek lines of the machine with a smidge more enthusiasm. 'I'm fine.' Her gaze narrowed on the relaxed-looking pilot writing something on a clipboard.

'Something wrong?' Seth quietly asked, a whisper in her ear.

'He's not wearing a uniform.' Lena managed to block her shiver. All pilots wore uniforms, didn't they?

Seth laughed. Lena's toes curled in her mules; that sound got her every single time.

'I don't require any of my staff to wear uniforms,' he eventually said when sober enough. 'We're not at school any more.'

'He's your personal pilot.' The penny dropped.

'To fly my personal plane, yes.'

'If you're trying to impress me it isn't going to work,' Lena bluffed. 'I'm surrounded by stupidly rich sportsmen, remember.'

'I know.' He shrugged, but his eyes twinkled.

And she knew, too, that not one of those stupidly rich sportsmen were wealthy enough to have their own set of planes in their own hangar with their own pilot on the pay-roll. 'So where are we flying to?'

'Auckland.'

'Seth—' she turned to him in disbelief '—there are a zillion commercial flights to Auckland every day. Can't you lower yourself to sit on a plane with ordinary members of the public? What about your carbon footprint?'

'This was a last-minute thing. All those flights were booked.'

He had the grace to look a teensy bit embarrassed. But she didn't believe all those flights were booked.

'I employ people, you know,' he said. 'Mike mightn't have a job if it weren't for me.'

'You don't have to justify it to me, just to yourself.'

'I sleep okay at night.' He grinned then.

She took a quick step forward and turned on tiptoe to face him front on. 'Really?'

'Okay, last night I didn't.'

Because he'd missed her? Just the thought seduced her heart into skipping a beat.

'I'm not looking forward to this meeting today.' His eyes teased.

'Oh, that's what kept you tossing and turning?' She didn't have that excuse.

The jet was small but luxurious. Only four seats in the back—two on each side, facing each other, with a table in between.

'I can usually get a lot of work done when we're in the air.' But he stowed the bag that clearly contained his laptop. And after take-off he swung round the table to squeeze next to her. Given the width of the seats it wasn't a problem.

'What about your work?'

'I need to do this more.'

Lena felt as if she were flying through heaven when he

kissed her. Sweetness poured into her, soothing the last sores from his standing her up the night before. Only then he sighed and moved back to the seat opposite. 'I have *got* to get my head together.'

'Important meeting?'

'Yeah.' He sighed the answer, already distracted as he scrolled through his PDA. 'And I'm really behind.'

Once they landed his distraction increased. He spent the entire taxi ride to the centre of town on his phone.

'I have to go straight into a meeting,' he said as they pulled up outside a hotel. 'An hour or so initially. But you wanted to shop, right? So meet me back here and we'll eat, okay?'

'Okay,' she supposed. She didn't know why it bothered her. He was here to work, after all, but she was being sent off already?

When she returned she found him waiting for her in the foyer with several men. He made quick introductions but it was clear the men were there to lunch, too.

'I can meet you later…' she said, to make it easy for him, despite her inner disappointment.

But Seth shook his head. 'No, stay and eat with us.'

She put on her professional smile and chattered her way through it. She knew how to interact with boardroom types like these. It was part of her job. Sure enough, the minute they learned where she worked, it was all on—nothing made highly successful businessmen more animated than behind-the-scenes rugby stories.

After a good half-hour of humorous anecdotes, conversation turned back to the deal on the table. Lena listened while Seth discussed his vision for the building he wanted to buy. She guessed it was a reiteration of his plans but she sensed how easily he'd won them over. With his charm, his infectious enthusiasm, mesmeric confidence he'd win over anyone. People couldn't help but agree with him. She wasn't sure it was all healthy.

He disappeared for another half-hour after lunch and she was shown to a suite on the top floor. Inexplicably her heart sank when she walked into the opulent room with the ridiculously big bed.

*I want to spend the day with you.*

His smooth invitation echoed, mocking her. Because, no, he didn't. Really he'd only wanted her to tag along so she was there when he had a spare five minutes to fool around.

It kicked right where she was most vulnerable. Reminding her of the time her ex had taken her away for a fun weekend. Only, once there it had turned out he had a conference to go to. It hadn't been 'til later that she realised the conference was the cover he'd used for his wife. And that the reason he was so keen to spend 'quality alone time' with her was because he didn't want too many others seeing her with him. She'd been so naïve she'd thought it sweet that he ordered the most amazing room-service meals. That he'd booked her into private massage and beauty therapy treatments for the mornings when he was on session. Really, he was just keeping her presence quiet.

Today, as she'd been then, she was the bit of fluff in attendance. Seth didn't want her here other than for his frisky fix, right? It wasn't as if he'd told her anything about his work; she'd only learned brief details from others at the lunch. He hadn't asked her opinion on anything. Did he think he could keep her happy with occasional scraps of sexual attention?

She flicked aimlessly through one of the glossy magazines on the table. High fashion and how-to guides didn't soothe or offer any perspective. She couldn't enjoy this as breezily any more. She wanted this to be more. But it wasn't and it wouldn't ever be.

Seth strode into the room, stripping off his tie and stuffing it in his pocket. 'I'm sorry if it was boring at lunch.'

That didn't help her mood. Did he think she'd been bored because she was some brainless babe who didn't understand the meaning of the word *acquisition*?

Despite her brewing temper, Lena couldn't tear her eyes from him—the baring of his body was always worthy of her attention. But to her surprise the rest of his clothes stayed on and he stayed near the door that he'd left open.

'Come on, let's get out of here,' he said. 'I'm dying for some fresh air.'

He didn't want to stay in here with that giant bed?

She had to walk quickly to keep pace with him as he crossed the foyer of the hotel and went out straight into a waiting taxi.

'Where are we going?' she finally got enough breath to ask.

'Somewhere more fun.'

Straight back to the airport? But it wasn't to the jet that he led her this time, but a helicopter.

'Don't worry.' He snaked a strong arm round her waist and guided her on board. 'I promise it's a professional, full-time pilot at the controls.'

'Where are we going?' she asked as the rotor blades whirred.

'The beach.'

It was only a twenty-five-minute flight to isolated paradise on the coast north of Auckland. Only two minutes more before they were both barefoot and splashing in the shallows.

'Thanks for coming today. I'm sorry it's been dull 'til now.' He smiled ruefully. 'I didn't want to come. Thought I could get away with conference calls from Christchurch. But I got pressured last night, which was why I was late to yours. When you said you had today off I thought I'd bring you with me. I couldn't wait for the meeting to be over.' He lifted her hand and kissed the back of it.

'So you could do this again?' She watched his face, couldn't help her insecurity. Had he just wanted a plaything at break time?

'There's a part of me that always wants to do this.' His lips tickled as he chuckled. 'But I wanted to bring you to this beach. And I have to confess it occurred to me mid-morning that you could help lighten up that lunch. And you did. I can't believe you got all their names after one quick intro and then totally entertained them like that. Can't tell you how much I appreciated it.'

His words released the ends of the bitter knot that had been forming. Why had she thought for even a second that Seth was anything like her jerk ex? He'd never tried to hide her away—he took her out all the time, he'd even introduced her to his business associates and now even sounded as if he was *proud* of her. She mentally shook herself. She thought she'd tamed her insecurities, but sometimes they snuck up when she least expected and screamed so loud she couldn't see straight.

But she knew why the doubts had found their way in today and why they'd made her so annoyed last night. She was falling all the more for Seth and it scared her. This wasn't staying as the light affair she'd thought she could handle. But maybe, just maybe, it would all work out okay. A seed of hope had just been sown. He hadn't wanted her for a mere thrill today, he'd wanted her *company*.

Only, along with the burst of happiness that that knowl-edge brought, concern came, too. 'Why were you so wor-ried about the meeting?' She'd never have picked him to be anxious, yet he'd clearly been unwilling and she couldn't understand why. 'You had all of them eating out of your hand.'

He laughed and squeezed her hand lightly. 'They only want to stay onside so I invest in some other things they've got on.'

'No, they were really impressed with your ideas. Not just your money.'

He glanced at her, a small smile tilting his lips before he kissed her hand again. 'I'm glad you think so.'

'So what was the problem, then?' Because clearly something had bothered him about the trip today.

'It wasn't the meeting.' He looked out to the empty horizon. 'It was the location. I grew up in Auckland.'

'Really?' She'd assumed he was a Christchurch kid, he seemed so entwined in the city.

'Yeah, and I know it's pathetic but I don't like coming back. Lots of unhappy memories. I've avoided it for years. Avoided my dad.'

'But I thought he was…'

'Dead, yeah. A year ago. Complications from the flu.'

'I'm sorry.'

He barely shrugged.

It was beyond obvious that they hadn't been close. It augmented her sympathy; he'd lost his chance to fix whatever had happened to cause this bitterness between them.

'He was a bastard.'

She flinched. That one descriptor and the superficial dismissiveness with which he said it revealed far more than a five-minute speech could. The underlying harsh hurt throbbed. She knew that, no matter how grown up you got, some things could still rub raw. Even when you thought you had an impenetrable scab covering an old wound, sometimes the smallest thing could just rip it right off.

'He walked out when I was fourteen,' he said quietly. 'It

was a really rough time before he left.' His shrug and almost smile didn't minimise the unease she sensed in him.

'What happened?'

His attempt to smile failed. 'Another woman is what happened.'

'He had an affair?' Lena's body temperature plummeted.

'With a manipulative number way nearer my age than his. She got pregnant.'

'Did she have the baby?' Lena uncurled her fingers so he'd let her hand go. She wanted to hide how clammy her palms had just got.

'That's how she got him to go back to her. He'd told Mum it was over and that he was staying. I thought it was all going to be okay—that they'd got through it. He was better, more involved, working. But six months later he told us his lover was pregnant and that he was leaving for good. It was more of a shock than when he'd first admitted the affair.'

'Oh, Seth.' Her heart sank.

'She was three months pregnant. He said seeing her again had been a one-off. A mistake because she'd been so devastated after he'd ended it. And now she was too vulnerable to manage on her own.' He shook his head derisively. 'She'd done whatever she had to, to catch and keep him.'

'You think she got pregnant on purpose?' His words scraped her skin, leaving her nerves and heart so exposed.

From the poisonous mood in the hotel room before she'd sailed to paradise, only to drop into a corrosive horror now. This was worse than her worst nightmare.

'Of course she did. It was the killer for my mum. She wanted more kids, but for whatever reason it didn't happen. I was it.'

'So she had the baby?'

'A boy. They married. And my feckless, charming father finally got his act together. They lived in Auckland. Moved into the home that had once been mine and Mum's, too, and left us with nothing. Tainted the whole damn town.'

Lena's heart blistered. 'How old is your half-brother?'

'I'm not sure, early teens maybe?'

She could tell from his eyes he knew exactly how old the kid was, he just didn't want to think about it.

'Have you ever met him?' she pressed anyway, her own demons pushing inside her.

'I had to visit a few times when I was a teen until I point-blank refused. I saw him at the funeral. We didn't chat.'

'You don't want to know him?'

'Why would I?'

'Because he's your half-brother.'

'He's not.' Seth shrugged. 'We have no real connection. And I sure as hell don't want anything to do with Rebecca Walker.'

Rebecca Walker. The name somehow made her real—and Lena felt so sorry. 'That's who that letter was from,' she said, suddenly making the connection. 'The other day. I thought it was odd that you chucked it because the sender had the same surname as you. R. Walker.'

'She only has the same surname because she married my father.'

'Why'd she write to you?' Lena's nerves pulled tight.

'Money,' he grunted.

Lena watched his barriers shut down—his face expressionless, his stance rigid on the sunny beach. 'But you don't actually know because you didn't open the letter.'

'Why would I?'

'You're not even curious?'

'No.'

From the uncompromising response she knew there was no point telling him he should be. He was too frozen to want to know. But what if something was wrong? Surely the woman wouldn't go to the trouble of writing to an estranged stepson without a good reason. His ruthless dismissiveness struck an ice-cold blade of fear into her. She understood his anger, she understood how hurt he must have been, but she hoped he could understand there might be another side to an age-old story. 'You know, it's not always the other woman who starts an affair,' she said nervously. 'Sometimes the married guy instigates it.'

'You're defending her?' His eyes widened.

'I just don't think one party is ever wholly to blame.' She dug her toes into the sand, trying to hide her discomfort. 'Sometimes a woman might be seduced. Your dad lied, Seth. Maybe he kept on lying. Maybe he'd been seeing her the whole time.'

'But she was the one who got herself knocked up so he felt like he couldn't abandon her.'

'It usually takes two to get pregnant.' She wished the water washing over her feet could wash away her festering wounds. But they just kept on stinging.

'Your parents are still happily married, right?' he said roughly. 'It's not something you can really comment on unless you've lived through it.'

But she had lived through it. She knew all about extramarital affairs. About flip-flopping emotions and false promises. About lies, counter lies and self-deception. And desperation.

The revelation about Seth's parents crushed the fledgling fantasy that this could be more than a fling for her and him. Now she knew he'd never be able to understand. She'd heard the scorn when he talked about his father's other woman. No shades of grey—Seth was black and white all the way.

She'd made some huge mistakes and she'd been trying so hard to move on and not make those mistakes again. Not to be the immature, attention-starved, vulnerable girl who'd messed up so royally. And she'd been succeeding. But she didn't think Seth would understand how her past had happened. Her affair with a married man had been more about her need to be wanted than her really wanting the man himself. It had been the attention—for the first time feeling that someone thought she was special, rather than feeling anything terribly special herself.

With Seth it was all different. With Seth it was all about her deepening feelings for him. Her incredible desire to be near his laughter, his light, his whole self. And that desire was expanding—she wanted to be part of his life, to share it all with him. She didn't want to give him up.

But soon she would have to. She couldn't hide her past for ever and she knew that the second he found out, it would be over.

## CHAPTER ELEVEN

LATER in the week, after more out-of-town meetings, Seth told Mike he wanted to fly back to Christchurch that evening, after all. He knew he should spend the night in Wellington—he had more meetings tomorrow. But now, last minute, he didn't want to. He'd fly back in the morning. And then back to Christchurch again in the afternoon in time for the game. Screw the carbon footprint. He'd plant some trees on a station somewhere.

He hadn't spent a night away in days. And there was only one green-eyed-brunette reason for that. A night away should have been good, would have been sensible, would have been a test. But he failed it gladly. Because he wanted nothing more than to be back with her as soon as possible. He didn't copilot as he sometimes did. Instead he sat in the cabin and stared into space. Trying to work out what the hell he thought he was doing.

He knew what she wanted—a man who was one hundred per cent there for her. Who'd pay her the attention she'd never got from her folks. He'd seen her mother's Facebook page in the weekend when they'd been playing on the computer. Lena hadn't been exaggerating. In all the photos of her siblings and their achievements, there was only the one of Lena—with Cliff Richard. She'd tried to laugh it off but he'd seen her face in that unguarded split second when she'd realised there were no other shots of her in the online album. She'd been hurt. And then resigned, as if she shouldn't have expected anything else. That was when she'd tried to laugh. But he didn't think it was all that funny.

Beautiful inside and out, she shouldn't be left in the shade. Like most flowers she needed full sun to bloom. The caring sweetheart had given so much more than she'd got back from her family. She deserved more from them. Deserved more than the little he could give her, too.

She needed absolute attention, utter security. And though she never mentioned it, had even once denied it, he knew that for her that would eventually mean marriage.

His lungs tightened. He could never offer her that. He knew what a farce it was. It trapped people into staying together for longer than they should. It produced kids only to mess them up.

He wasn't ever going to marry, never have kids. So given their opposing future ideals, he knew he shouldn't be hanging around her now. He should be backing away so she was free to meet the guy who'd be all good for her. She was a team player who liked to support others—but who needed someone to support her needs just as much. Whereas he liked to live alone and never rely on another. Never feel the burden of being relied upon for emotional fulfilment—for he was fully aware he'd fail to carry it. Hell, he couldn't even get her to tell him about the guy who'd done her over. It shouldn't bother him, but it did. He couldn't end this until he knew it all. And even more stupidly, his big place felt too bare and empty now; he liked her lushly furnished rooms better. So when he landed, well past midnight, he quietly crept into her bed.

'Seth?' She was curled in a cosy ball like a cat—but he wasn't lulled into thinking she was harmless. She was more sleeping lioness than kitten.

'Shh, it's late.' He kissed her lips—a chaste, soft kiss. He kissed her cheek, her brow. Tenderness washed over him, soothing down the embers of desire.

She mumbled something; he didn't catch it. But he knew she was happy, he saw the soft smile, heard the sleepy chuckle. It touched him. He pulled her back against him, gently pressing a light kiss on the tip of her ear, the edge of her cheek. She stirred again, muttered something else and then relaxed, warm against him.

Long into the night, he lay awake. Holding her softness close, listening to her smooth breathing. Her husky whisper echoed round his head, sending vitality—entwined with terror—pulsing through his soul. Had she really just muttered those three little words?

He'd heard them before, from other women when they were wide awake. He hadn't believed them. They'd wanted his success and status rather than him. But Lena didn't want to feed off his success. Lena was working out her own meaning of that word. Lena wasn't like them. She wasn't like anyone else he'd met. How he felt now was totally foreign, too.

Now he wished he'd stayed away.

Lena woke, amazed to find him profoundly asleep in her bed. He wasn't supposed to be here. He was supposed to be in Wellington. But he'd obviously wanted to come home—to her. She lay quietly, looking at his beautifully relaxed expression. He was so handsome. She thought back, remembering now that she'd felt his weight on the bed in the middle of the night, that she'd turned and cuddled into his warmth, that she'd been so pleased she'd said…

*Oh, no.*

She carefully eased out of bed so she didn't wake him. Had a shower in which she squeezed her eyes tight against the tears. It was one thing to admit her weakness to herself, it was another to admit it to him. Because she also remembered his response to her declaration—his utter silence.

The hour before work ticked away. She dressed, breakfasted and still he snoozed on. In the silence she formulated a plan. She'd pretend she'd never said it. Pretend she'd been asleep. Pretend that nightmare reality had been a dream.

'Why aren't you out of bed yet? Don't you have deals to make or something?' She put her hand on his foot and jiggled it. 'In *Wellington*?'

Zero reaction.

She pulled the curtains open and jabbed at his prone form again.

Finally he groaned. 'It took ages to get to sleep.' Bleary-eyed, he rubbed his hand over his face. 'Lena—' He broke off.

'Mmm?' She picked up her bag, and glanced at her reflection, needing a second before facing him. 'What?'

No answer. She turned. For a second he met her gaze, then he looked away. Sitting up, he covered his body with a sheet. He never did that.

'I've got to go,' she said lamely, dying inside.

He couldn't look at her. And he didn't answer.

'You'll have to let yourself out.' She sprinted to the door. 'I'm late already.'

Seth slumped back down the bed and stared at the ceiling, still hearing the husky whisper. Maybe it had been a dream. He'd been that tired. He was still tired. And totally out of sorts. Just then she'd escaped as fast as she could. He didn't know if that meant she remembered or not. Either way she was hiding from him and he didn't like it. He flung the sheet up over his face and closed his eyes, trying to slip back into a half sleep. Except he ached all over. Maybe he was coming down with flu.

He should have stayed away last night. He should stay away tonight instead. He needed some space to think clearly but there was no getting out of going to the Knights' home game. He had to be there for the boys. It was their big reward for turning up to the training and for turning up to school this week.

He lay, breathing in her soft scent, and finally faced it. What he'd wanted, why he was feeling this disgruntled— this *disappointed*. He'd wanted her to say it again. He'd wanted her to wake and to say it again and to mean it.

He'd never wanted that from anyone, never wanted to want it. But it had snuck up on him. She had. His heart thundered in both horror and frustration. Because now he had to deal with a whole day away, then a whole evening of being social. He showered and dressed and headed back to the airport. He didn't text or call. Because he needed to see her face to face. Once all the day's obligations were done, he'd get her alone and up close and, cautious as he suddenly was, he'd see what happened.

Lena didn't pay attention to the game. The Knights won, of course, but that was inevitable. Seth was in the VIP stand with his boys. Even the ones who believed they were literally too cool for school looked blown away. Andrew and Dion were with them, too. The boys were getting the full preferential treatment—dinner before the match, dessert halfway through in the private suite, plus the chance to mingle with the Knights at the after-match function now. Watching from a distance, she chatted with other guests and truly understood what a mess she'd made of it. She'd done it again, fallen for someone who didn't want the same thing as her. And this time she'd fallen in love for real.

He didn't feel the same way. Her half-dozy declaration had killed it. He wouldn't even hold her gaze across the room. She'd tried, sent him a smile when she'd caught him glancing at her. But he'd blanked it—looked away as fast as possible and then actually turned his back.

She knew he was a better man than her ex. He didn't lie, didn't cheat. He had his own code. But he had faults, too. It hurt her to see him being so nice to those kids tonight when he was blanking his own blood—his half-brother. He couldn't forgive. So Lena knew just how to end it with him. Because, as she'd promised herself from the start, *she* would be the one to call time. And she had to now. He wasn't ever going to change for her.

By now the Knights had come up from the change room. Suited up in their finery, they were busy doing obligatory chats with the sponsors and guests before they hit the clubs in town and celebrated the way they really wanted to. A group were paying special attention to Andrew and the boys. Lena couldn't bear to watch any more. Her duty was almost over for the night and she'd snatch a breather now. She slipped out of the room into the cooling air. Other than the crowd in the glassed-in corporate boxes, the stadium was now empty. The audience had drained away, the cleaners had already swept round collecting the plastic cups and wrappers left strewn over the seating. She walked down the steps of the private stand and stood at the railing—literally bracing herself.

'Lena?'

So he'd followed.

'If your half-brother was in a mess like those boys up there, would you help him?' she asked without preamble.

The late-summer night was light enough for her to see his immediate frown as he leant on the railing. 'Why would you think he's in trouble?'

'What if that's why she's writing to you?'

He laughed—roughly. 'Lena, trust me, it's probably

money. It's amazing, the people who crawl out of the wood-work claiming some kind of kinship or pleading some sob story when they know you're wealthy.'

'Well, what if it is? What if they're struggling like you and your mum struggled? Would you want him to go through the kind of hardship you went through?'

His frown was thunderous. 'He'll never go through what I went through.'

'Seth.' Her heart pleaded for him to be more sympathetic. 'He's lost his father.'

'I lost my father, too,' he said coldly. 'A long time ago.'

'About the same age as he did.' Lena nodded. 'What if he needs a decent man in his life to help him out now? Or do you want him to have to fight through it, too?'

Seth abruptly straightened. 'Lena, this is pointless. You're never going to understand—'

'No, *you* won't,' she interrupted harshly. 'You'll *never* understand.'

'Understand what?'

She turned and hit him as he'd once told her to. Only, words could wound so much more than fists. 'How I came to have an affair with a married man. How for almost a year I was his mistress. How I tried to break up a marriage.'

He stared, his eyes widening to huge. *'What?'* He sounded half-strangled.

'You heard. I was the other woman interfering in a mar-riage, Seth. I tried to break them up. I did everything I could.'

She'd been so pathetically needy. She'd given up so much when she'd been waiting for him to give her all he'd said he would. Lost more when it had all come crashing down. The friends she'd ditched to be available for him then had ditched her. Her parents had been appalled. The only thing she'd been able to do was get the hell out of that town and start afresh.

She'd promised herself that she'd never make that kind of mistake again. Yet here she was putting out for a guy who wanted nothing more from her. Allowing herself to be basically used because her stupid heart had got ideas above its station. And it was so much worse this time. Because this time she'd truly fallen. It wasn't about being the one chosen over another, about being picked first for once in her life. It had been that before—all about being the woman who won. And she hadn't.

She had her eyes wide open now, no more naïve fantasy. There was no other woman here. Only her but she still wasn't going to win. The pleasure she got from being with Seth was deep and real. She knew his faults. She knew he was arrogant and proud but also unforgiving. She loved him anyway. But she had to shatter it because *he* didn't love her. And that wasn't going to change.

'They were married and I was the other woman,' she said harshly. 'I'm the temptress tart, Seth. I'm the kind of woman you hate.'

He'd frozen. Something hard glittered in his eyes—cutting her heart like diamond-tipped blades. Suddenly she couldn't resist trying to explain it—not excuse it, but explain it.

'I know *exactly* how it happened and he was no lily-white old fool who got trapped,' she said in a rush. 'He chased me. In the beginning he chased so hard. He told me he was separated. I wouldn't touch him until he'd said the divorce was under way. He even showed me a lawyer's letter. It was fiction. He chased and chased and I was stupidly flattered. Once he'd got what he wanted, that's when he began to cool, but by then I didn't see it. I was seduced by the attention. I wanted it all and more. I believed he loved me. I believed his promises.' She'd been a naïve, needy idiot and she wasn't going to be that girl any more. 'I'm not going to be used like that again. And that's what's happening here. I can't keep seeing you when you can't give me what I want.'

'*I'm* not cheating you, Lena.' His knuckles were white on the railing—only half a metre along from her own bloodless fists.

'Not with another woman. But your "my parents screwed up so I'll never make the mistake of getting married myself" line is a convenient excuse for serial monogamy and not committing. That way you get to play the field in a kind of code that's acceptable to you. That way you don't have to admit all you're really interested in from me is short-term sex.'

'We never made promises. *You* wanted a series of one-night stands.'

'That's right and I was wrong. One day you'll meet some woman who has it all and you'll offer everything you've said you never will. But that woman's not me. It'll never, *ever* be me.'

She paused to draw breath, but also because she had some stupid weak hope that he'd interrupt her now and shout that she was wrong and that she *was* that woman.

Of course he didn't. He just stood pale, his chest rising and falling fast, his jaw clamped.

'You make that excuse to women like me because you know we don't have whatever it is that would hold your interest for long.' She tossed her head back, summoning the last of her defiance. 'I refuse to be so needy again. I deserve more than this.'

'But you were the one who stipulated this was purely physical in the first place.'

'Because I wanted you,' she shouted. 'But stupidly I want

*more.* I thought I could control that but I can't and you're not ever going to give it to me.'

She was better on her own than waiting to be ditched. Than giving up her heart and not getting his in return. 'Admit it, Seth, you don't want more from me.'

He didn't deny it. He just stared at her, just looked blown away. It made her all the more angry. She wished he would say it. Wished he'd end this as decisively as she knew he could. Instead *she* had to push it. To sever the last thin thread of attraction.

'You know you could never trust me.' She acted up, playing the man-stealing vixen she'd been labelled. 'You'd always wonder. I did it once—knowingly slept with a guy who belonged to another woman. A married man. I lied to everyone. Really well.' Most of all to herself. 'I *deliberately* tried to take him away from his wife. How could you ever think I'd be faithful? Who's to say I haven't been already with you?'

He'd gone paler. Good.

'You loathe infidelity. Now you're looking at the queen of it. Someone as virtuous as you must surely hate me. After all, it's always the tart who's to blame.'

She hated him then for the heavy judgment in his absolute silence. 'But you know what, Seth? You're not that perfect, either.' She turned the venom from herself to him. 'There were shades of grey in what you did with me. You slept with me that first night despite knowing it would make things awkward for me the next day when you came calling for your little favour. But you wanted your good time and you got it and damn the little question of ethics or fair play. You push everything as close to the edge as you can. And you parade your independence like it's so damn great, but it's just a mask for selfishness and an inability to *care.* You're so closed off, so unforgiving that you can't even bring yourself to find out if your own flesh and blood is okay. Well, *that's* not okay. And I'm through with you.' She stopped, stared, her fury spent.

He stood so still—like granite. Unfeeling. Uncaring.

Tears blinded her. Desperate to hide them, she turned and took to the stairs as if a monster were at her heels.

'Excuse me.' She pushed past some rugby player standing in the doorway and slipped through the crowd out to the exit corridor on the other side.

She'd done it. Ended everything between them. And all it had taken was the truth.

A kaleidoscope of images whirled in Seth's head. Confused emotions rioted in his body. He stared at the empty stadium stairs. Dazedly thought how she'd taken them three at a time to get back into the VIP suite. He was totally shocked and it was taking too long to process the last four-minute nightmare. Of all the things he'd thought might happen tonight, it sure as hell hadn't been that. He breathed, trying to get the oxygen hit that might make the smothering fog clear. But it didn't. All he had were questions and questions and a hellish bad ache compressing his chest. She'd struck when he'd least expected it, where he'd least expected. She'd hurled a mangled mess of past and present at him. Rejected him. Then run for good measure.

He swore as anger rose—burning, blinding, bloody bitter anger. How the hell was he supposed to react when she didn't even give him a second to think, let alone answer? He might be selfish, but she was the biggest coward he'd ever met.

It was only a minute before he followed her. But in the crowded room he instantly sensed the void.

She'd already gone.

# CHAPTER TWELVE

IF IT had just been sex, living without it would be easy. Lena had lived without sex for months. And if sex was all she'd wanted, she could get it elsewhere. She could say yes to that newest recruit and spend the night with a beautiful, fit body.

But it was so much more than sex. Sitting on her sofa, Lena curled into a ball and cried. She cried because she missed him. She cried because what she had to offer wasn't enough. She cried because he didn't have the humanity she needed him to. He didn't seem to have the same need as anyone else—to be part of a team. To want support and companionship and understanding.

The night dragged. She couldn't sleep for that last little hope that he'd call by—that he'd come after her.

He didn't.

She made work extremely busy, begging extra tasks from Dion. For three days she basically lived at the stadium. She'd blocked Seth's number from her phone, set his email address as spam so she had no idea if he tried to contact her. But she was certain he wouldn't now. He must hate her. She never mentioned him to Dion, who never mentioned him back. She'd get over him—one minute at a time.

Wednesday morning she walked out of the tunnel on her way to deliver a parcel to the coach. The boys were training on the pitch already. Her tight control on her thoughts slipped—there was no amateur extra out on the field today. No gorgeous guy laughing with a bunch of kids in his grey tee. Memory washed over her, a powerful wave that she closed her eyes to endure. So she didn't see the rope lying across her path. But she sure as hell felt the concrete.

She blinked and saw a montage of faces moving above her like a wobble board. She quickly shut her eyes again, screwing them tight because the motion-sickness thing was still with her.

'Lena? Lena? *Lena?*' One rugby player seemed to be uncertain if she was who she was.

'Get Gabe.' Someone else, possibly Ty.

'I'm fine,' she said firmly, keeping her eyes shut.

'You're not. Don't move.'

She had no intention of moving. It'd be great if she could slink off and hide, but it was totally impossible.

'Is it just your head hurting?'

Actually the only thing hurting was her heart. The rest of her was numb. 'I don't know.'

'Can you feel this?' Impersonal hands pressed on her ankles, up to her knees, then shifted to her arms.

She nodded slightly before wincing as pain suddenly pounded in her temple.

'Up we go.'

Someone picked her up and held her close to his chest. Not the right guy.

'I'm so embarrassed.' She'd never tripped in her heels before. Now she'd given the guys real reason to hassle her about them.

'Forget it.'

It was Gabe carrying her. If she had a penchant for moody dark-eyed men, she'd have fallen quite easily for Doctor Gabe months ago as so many of those dancers had, but she preferred the blue-eyed, make-you-laugh type. He put her on a bench in the change room and made her hold a cloth to her head. She lifted it away a second and felt sick when she saw it was blood-soaked already. Ty and Jimmy squatted down in front of her while Gabe went fussing for something in his bag of gear.

'You need us to do anything, Lena?' Jimmy asked. 'Don't want us to take someone down in a heavy head-high tackle or anything?'

She looked at them, caught between mortification at them knowing she was heartbroken and a bit of gratitude because they cared.

'Oh, boys,' she half growled. 'I can take care of myself.'

'We don't like to see you hurt. And, uh—' Ty gestured to his head '—not just there.'

'That's really nice of you but...' She trailed off as acid tears pricked her eyes. 'Oh, hell, that is really nice of you.'

'You're our bossy sister, you know?'

She nodded and instantly stopped with a wince. 'And you're all annoying brothers.'

'He's a fool.'

Yeah, they knew. Of course they'd all have seen what was going on the last couple of weeks. And what wasn't now. 'Can we just forget about it and act like normal?'

'Sure.' Ty nodded.

'You guys need to focus on your game. And I've stuff to do. We'll do that, okay?' But they'd just slid the smallest cushion beneath her battered heart. They cared. They appreciated her. And that was a smear of salve that she really needed right now.

She had a great job. She had value. She'd pick herself up, dust herself down and get on with it. She'd work harder still. As agonising as it was, she knew now she could do the right thing. She was stronger, wiser, more capable. And maybe one day, she might meet someone who'd appreciate her, know her faults and love her anyway.

One day a long way off from today.

The change-room door hit the wall with a bang. 'Where is—?'

Lena stared, clutching the bloodied rag to her head as Seth stopped talking and strode to where she sat. His presence ripped away that cushion and smashed her raw heart back onto jagged rocks for seagulls to peck at.

'Seth was with me when the boys buzzed for Gabe.' Dion hovered in the doorway.

With Dion. Not here to see her. Her hope's last feeble flare was shot down just like that.

'I'm fine.' Lena forced a fake smile. 'I'm fine.' Could they all please leave now? Especially him.

It was only Ty and Jimmy who backed out, sending Seth glowering glances before taking Dion with them. Lena was acutely aware he was too busy staring at her to see them.

'That's a hell of a gash. Does she need stitches?' Seth whirled and looked at Gabe, who now had his gloves on and his oversized scary-looking staple gun at the ready. 'Should you be doing this?'

Lena saw Gabe's eyes kindle at the doubt in Seth's tone.

'In between the sprained ankles and torn tendons I do a spot of stitching, as well,' the doctor said coolly.

'But this is her face.'

Gabe stood tall. 'I've done plenty of facial cuts and there are no scars on any of my patients. It would ruin the calendar.' He knelt before Lena. 'So there'll be no scar on you, either, sweets. Not from me.'

The resulting silence was so pointed it could have cut lead.

Gabe worked carefully, quietly. Lena was frozen stiff. Seth stood slightly to the side, not taking his eyes off her.

She couldn't let herself pay attention to it. He was here to see Dion. Not her.

Finally Gabe rose and peeled off his gloves. 'There you go, watch for a headache because there might be a touch of concussion. So don't be alone tonight.'

She really wished he hadn't said that in front of Seth. She smoothed down her skirt and forced her legs to hold steady as she stood. She didn't want to have to take any assistance.

Gabe grabbed his bag and left the room. Lena breathed slowly a couple of times to make sure she could get out of there without keeling over again. Seth still just stood watching—too close. She had to break the dreadful silence somehow.

'You had a meeting with Dion?'

'You've been working hard?' He asked his question at the same time as she did.

She waited a second and then answered, 'Very.' She straightened her shoulders and took firm steps to the door. 'It's going well.'

'Great,' he clipped, suddenly looking everywhere but at her. 'I guess I'll see you...'

It was just a polite word of farewell that he didn't even finish. There was certainly no offer to keep an eye on her possibly concussed self.

No. There was no depth behind that initial moment of concern. No hidden meaning. Fighting back tears, Lena carefully walked back up to her office. She closed the door, thankful for the ton of work on her desk that she could bury her whole self in.

Seth strode—okay, sprinted—out of there. Bitter-tasting spit filled his mouth. He was so near to literally spilling his guts. It wasn't her bloodied head he found horrific, but her hard shell—her unresponsive expression.

He hated it. Wished he hated her. He'd tried for days to push her out of his mind. He'd flown out of the city and worked and worked and worked. But it hadn't worked. As soon as he'd landed back in Christchurch he'd come straight to the stadium and got upstairs in time to hear that Gabe was needed. For Lena. He'd sprinted to that change room and his heart had both leapt and stopped at the sight of her.

He desperately wanted to talk to her but one look told him the timing was impossible. It was horribly obvious that she didn't want him there. Didn't need him. So cold. That hurt more than anything ever had or could. She'd ended it and she was fine about it. How could she be the same woman who'd whispered her love so sweetly late that night? Or did she whisper that to anyone who happened to be in her bed?

No. He couldn't believe that. But nor could he believe her confession about her affair, either. Hurt surged higher, because she'd never have told him about it if it weren't true. So now he wanted to erase the whole damn thing. He wanted not to care.

But he couldn't stop.

He was almost at his car when he saw Ty, the captain, walking towards him.

'Is Lena okay?' Ty asked shortly.

'Yeah.' Seth glanced up. The other player from the change room was watching close, clearly the back-up. 'She seems fine.'

'You think?' Ty asked, all ominous.

But that was fine, because Seth felt like fighting. Bare knuckles and blood. 'Doing the big-brother act?'

'What makes you think I feel brotherly about Lena?' Ty glared back. 'She turned me down like she did everyone else, but I meant it more than most. And she deserves some-one who can give her what she needs.'

'You think you know what she needs?' Seth *hated* this.

'Maybe I've got more of an idea than you.'

Seth didn't bother answering. Just got into his car, slammed the door and fired the engine, wanting to go faster than sound and burn the hell out. He couldn't bear the thought of that beautiful woman laughing at that guy's lame jokes the way she did at his. Couldn't bear the thought of her snuggled on a sofa with him and commentating her way through the replay of the day.

But she'd refused Ty. She'd refused all those boys. In the face of all those eligible offers, she'd taken up none. But she'd taken Seth on.

*Why?*

Within five minutes of getting to his apartment, he was bare-chested and bare-knuckled and beating the crap out of his punchbag. Trying to beat the bitter hurt out of his body. For the first time in three days he let himself listen to the arguments endlessly circling in his head.

He'd hated his father, but *loathed* his father's lover. So he hated that Lena had been the other woman like that. He hated that she'd lied and cheated. But he couldn't hate *her.*

Because didn't he know how it felt to be rejected? Didn't he know how awful it felt—not to be enough? His mother had never said anything to him direct, but late one miserable night as his parents' marriage had blown up he'd heard her on the phone to a friend. Bawling her eyes out, heartbroken that her husband's mistress was pregnant. Because she'd wanted more children. Because Seth wasn't enough for her. And not enough to save her marriage. So he'd learned he didn't have whatever it was necessary to make someone else happy. Nothing he'd done seemed to be enough. And he'd decided that if he was going to get on in this world, it had to be all his own doing. He wouldn't ever depend on another like that for happiness.

He punched harder. Because that old rule had taken a battering recently.

Lena had made mistakes but Seth could understand why. His father's abandonment had left him hungry for success, but Lena's neglect and constant inferior comparison to her super-siblings had left her hungry for approval, for love. That gnawing desire to be needed. And yeah, Seth understood Lena's need for parental approval or support. She was right. In the heart of every kid, that desire would always have a root. Even grown-up kids. Hadn't he, even in a tiny part of his heart, wanted that? He'd wanted it from his father and it was too late now. Didn't he want his mum to take what he offered her—even just the damn money so he could feel as if he supported her and was somehow of use? So much for his supposed emotional independence.

So he couldn't judge, could he? Because he was as damaged as she. She was right; he was selfish. He wanted his fun his own way. But she was wrong, too. His not wanting commitment wasn't entirely a convenient excuse. It was grounded in fear. Because if he lost all his money, his status, even his damn fitness, would any woman still be interested? He doubted it. His own father hadn't stayed interested even as his success was blossoming.

So he protected his heart by keeping things casual and always being the one to end it. He saw now that Lena had tried to do the same. She'd tried to protect herself from him. That was why she'd said no after their first one-night stand. She was more emotionally aware than he and had feared she was headed for trouble if she messed with him much more. That hunt for self-protection had been at the root of her 'non-exclusive' offer. It had stemmed from her insecurity. She really did believe she didn't have enough to offer him.

So now? Where the hell did they go from here?

He smacked the bag, his fists sore, then raw, then heading

to numb. He stewed over her past. But in the end all he could think was that people made mistakes. And he wanted to know how she'd come to make hers. He had to try to understand. She had to help him do that. Because as flawed and fickle as she might once have been, he loved her. He wanted to be with her. And he wanted to convince her he could love her the way she needed to be loved. He wanted to be enough for her.

But given how insecure she was, he knew she needed more than words. She needed incontrovertible proof. So for her, and only for her, he'd consider the marriage deal. If she wanted the public ceremony and the piece of paper, he'd give her that. Hell, he could give her a really public declaration—he could do a huge public proposal. Bare his soul in a stadium full of people.

That would be big. And public. And manipulative.

Would she be able to say no in that arena even if she wanted to? Actually, knowing Lena she probably could. But he didn't want to do it to her anyway, didn't want to set her up so she felt pressured by an audience to answer a certain way. He wanted her to be completely free to make whatever decision was in her heart.

But before he could go forward with her, there was the past to resolve. As much as he didn't want to, he had to cut them free from her baggage—and his own.

Seth stopped punching. Yeah, there was that whole deal. The kid his father had chosen to be with. The one who had taken his place. Jason. Seth had been totally jealous of him. He'd met him a few times when his mother had made him visit his father in an attempt to maintain their father-son relationship. But his father had that new son—the screaming baby who'd grown into a cute toddler. The apple of his father's eye.

But that wasn't Jason's fault. Seth might be many things,

but he wasn't a monster. He didn't want the kid to suffer any more than he wanted any other kid to suffer. And he didn't want Jason to be as lonely as he felt now. He stalked to the table and rummaged underneath for the wastepaper bin that was still overflowing from the other week. Kicked so far under the table he'd forgotten about it. And not emptied. The letter was on top.

He skimmed it. So he'd been wrong and she'd been right. Again. It wasn't a request for money, but a request for him to get in touch with his brother. Rebecca knew Seth would never want to deal with her, but she was desperate for Jason. He'd been struggling since their father's death. Seth sighed deeply, trying to release the clamped feeling in his chest. He had no other siblings. No real experience of dealing with them. So he really didn't know how Lena coped with the whole competitive thing, but he knew she loved her siblings and supported them. He admired her for that. And there was more that he had to learn from her.

For the first time in his life he wanted a team-mate. Not just a support person, but someone fighting alongside him. He ached for her strength and loyalty and laughter. And her love.

But in love there were no guarantees. So he was going to have to man up to the most difficult challenge of his life.

## CHAPTER THIRTEEN

THE painkillers Gabe had given her weren't working. Her whole body felt heavy and sore and for the next hour she simply sat in her chair, utterly ineffective.

'I'm sending you home. I've called a car already.'

Lena jerked, her head pounded harder; she hadn't realised Dion was standing in her doorway. She had no idea how long he'd been standing there. But she didn't argue, for once recognising her own limitations and that she was right at the edge of them. Better for her to leave now rather than have a total meltdown at work. 'Thanks.'

By the time she'd gathered her gear and got down the stairs the car was at the front entrance. A big black one. Her heart shrivelled—she couldn't take this. But then the driver's door opened and it was Mike, the pilot, who got out. There was no one else in the car.

'What are you doing here?' She was too sore to put the polite smile on.

'Don't worry, Lena,' he said easily. 'I'm just taking you home.'

She hesitated but knew she was too spent to argue. So she just got in. Her heart thudded painfully. She hoped Seth wouldn't be there; she really didn't have the strength to face him. Never would. Her eyes watered and she blinked hard to keep her emotions buried.

But he was there, leaning against the wall next to her front door, shaded from the blazing midafternoon sun. As she walked up the path she heard Mike drive away.

'You know we have to talk,' he said as she neared.

She didn't unlock her door, couldn't bear to bring him into her home again. Instead she stopped and sat on the concrete steps leading to her deck. A half second later he moved, and sat beside her.

She kept her head bent, but she saw the backs of his hands as he hunched and rested his arms on his thighs. The skin across his knuckles was swollen and red and purple and smote her heart.

'Lena, I need you to tell me about it. I want to try to understand.'

The band of pain tightened round her head as she gingerly shook it.

'Tell me what happened,' he said softly, insistently. 'I want to know.'

'Why?' What was the point in rehashing her past mistakes? It was hardly going to redeem her. Why couldn't he just walk away and leave her to deal with it?

'Do you believe in love at first sight?' he asked.

She stared hard at the concrete but it went all blurry. Not only did she feel the pain pounding now, she heard it, too. 'Do you?'

'I didn't used to believe in love at all.'

Her head hurt. Her heart hurt. *Everything* hurt.

'It's been an adjustment.'

She didn't respond to that low drawl. Couldn't, daren't hope. Suddenly it was easier to think on her painful past than her possible future now.

'His name was Cam,' her voice rasped. 'He was my boss.'

Everything she'd said the other night had been true, but there had been things she hadn't said. Now her words dropped like stones, smashing the silence and all the possibilities that hovered in it. She bent her head. She didn't want to see his face. 'I'm so ashamed I did that to another woman.' The harshness dropped from her voice and she whispered instead. 'I was so naïve.'

She'd wanted to be loved so much. That desire had blinded her to the reality of the situation. Just for once she'd wanted to be treasured, made to feel special. She hadn't ever been special. She'd never shone at anything. And he'd made her feel as if she did.

'He chased me so hard,' she said sadly. 'He was older and in a senior position and I was flattered. He showered me with gifts. Everything a greeting-card lover should—flowers, chocolates, even jewellery. And attention. I fell for it. I'd get into work and there'd be an email waiting. The second I sat down the phone would go and it would be him on the end of the line—just to say hello. He'd come to my part of the office at any opportunity. I was so dazzled and young and stupid. And so lonely.'

And so used to being second best. It had taken nothing to make her fall into his arms. He hadn't even been that attractive, but he'd wanted her as no one else had ever wanted her. Chased as no one had ever chased. Paid her so much attention.

'I didn't know he was still with her, not when it started. He told me he was separated and filed for divorce.' But ignorance was no excuse. She should have found out sooner. She should have known that he hadn't left his wife as he'd said. She should never have believed a word of it.

'I wanted so badly to believe he liked me that I didn't believe it when I heard the truth. And by the time I did face it, I no longer cared about the rights or wrongs. He promised me he'd leave her. And I wanted to keep him.' In the end she'd left town. Crushed and humiliated and horrified. 'I never wanted to be the *other* woman. I wanted to be the *only* woman.'

'He seduced you.' Seth finally spoke.

'I didn't make it that difficult for him.' She wasn't entirely at fault, but she'd step up to take her share of the blame. 'And I didn't walk away when I should have.' She chewed on her lip. 'I *wanted* him to leave her for me. I wanted him to pick me over her. I wanted to come first. So I tried to break them up. I did everything I could to make him love me. I let him do anything he wanted to in the hope he'd love me for it. For months.' Her eyes watered. 'That's how pathetically needy I was.'

'It's not needy to want to be loved.'

'It's wrong to want to break up a marriage.'

'Is that what you really wanted?' he asked bluntly. 'Was it really even *him* you wanted? Or did you just want to win?'

And there it was. She, who'd never won a damn thing in her life—who'd been outsmarted and outsported by her siblings her entire life. Who'd never done whatever it was she needed to do to win her parents' attention. Who'd been the support act for ever....

'I wanted to win,' she said fiercely. 'I just wanted to win for once.' Her tears spilled. 'I was a bitch.'

'No,' he argued gently. 'You were young and hurt and nobody likes to feel rejected.'

She couldn't believe he was being this understanding. He wasn't angry at all, wasn't blaming her, was just listening. Seeming to see *why*. She stared hard, trying to contain the emotions exploding within her. The hope.

'How did it end?'

She winced and wiped her face. 'His wife got pregnant,' she whispered. 'I was so naïve I'd believed him when he said he wasn't sleeping with her. So it was then when I finally realised that he was never going to leave her like he'd said he would. He'd been telling me nothing but lies. He didn't want anything from me other than sex on tap. And I'd let myself be used. Begged for it, really. I know I did wrong. But I wanted to be loved so much and instead I lost everything—my friends, my job, my dignity.' She shook her head. That was when she'd finally fought back. 'I moved towns, worked really hard. Got this job and worked even harder and steered clear of men. I was working on getting myself together. On growing up. I was waiting for Mr Right. I was going to be strong. But then you came along.'

'I can't be Mr Right?'

She closed her eyes. 'You said yourself you weren't Mr Marry-Me, you were Mr Temptation. You were the guy I took one look at and simply had to have. The *only* guy it's been like that with. Attraction just slammed me in the gut. I thought I could get away with it—just once. But you wouldn't let it be once. And I didn't want to deny myself, either. I couldn't. Only, then I started to want so much more and I knew you never would.'

'Why wouldn't I?'

Because she wasn't the wonder woman who could break through his emotional-isolation policy. 'All we do is hot sex,' she said sadly. 'So what? That flame will snuff soon. You'll get bored, we'll go from shagging three times a night to three times a week and soon after you'll realise there's nothing else you see in me. In the end you'll go and find someone else who does give you something more. I can't sit by and wait for that to happen.'

He was very quiet. She glanced at him and flinched. Stunned to see his face had gone white, but that his eyes burned navy blue. Why was he looking so furious now when he hadn't before?

'You once asked why I'd been angry.' He barely moved his mouth as he spoke evenly. Too evenly. 'For me the cause is always the same. Hurt. A hurt that I don't want to feel, so I get angry to cover it. Right now I'm feeling angrier than I ever have.' He jerked to his feet, whirling to tower above her, his voice rising at the same time. 'How the hell can you say this is just sex?' His bruised fists clenched. 'Don't we laugh? Don't we talk? Don't we argue about stupid referee decisions? Don't we do a million things together that are simple and satisfying and not just sexual? Don't you dare deny that we have all that and more.'

'Of course—' She choked. Damn it, he knew she got everything, *wanted* everything from him.

He stopped. Suddenly dropped to his knees in front of her. 'Is it so hard to believe that I'd fall for you?' He looked up into her face, his anger suddenly extinguished. 'You have to have some faith in yourself. And in me.'

But she couldn't possibly believe he meant this. 'How can you forgive my past?'

He paused, looked down at the back of his hands. 'To be honest, I don't think I need to forgive you. I think you need to forgive yourself.'

Lena went hot and cold and stopped breathing.

'You're not letting yourself be open to me because you think you're not good enough? That you don't deserve it? Of course you do. You're amazing—you're funny and enthusiastic and smart and strong and beautiful. Why the hell wouldn't I want to be with you?'

'Seth.' She bit back the sob, the need to fling herself into his arms.

'You wanted to be put first but you won't believe it when it happens?'

'It's never happened before.' She only half joked.

'It was only a matter of time before it did. You don't even see it when it's staring you in the face. Half that rugby team would put you first in their lives if you'd given them the chance. But I'm glad you didn't. I'm glad it's me having to fight my way into that heart of yours.'

'You don't have to fight your way in,' she admitted helplessly. 'I told you it was one look. One single, half-second look.'

'So why can't you believe that it's the same for me?'

She still couldn't move. 'Will you be able to trust me?' she mumbled, knowing this fragile thing could never blossom without trust.

'Yes.'

'Why?'

'Because you're an intelligent person and you've learnt your lesson. You chose not to stay in a position where you believed you were going to be hurt again. You chose to end it with me because you thought your heart was in danger. And you weren't cheating. There was no one else but us. You're a different woman from the girl you were then. You're resilient and strong and determined to do the right thing. I've seen you with those guys. I know how professional you are with them. I know you wouldn't dream of jeopardising your job with any of them. But with me? You risked a lot for me right from the start. You were courageous with me then. Be courageous now.'

The dam burst inside her, flooding her with hope and love. She'd told him her greatest shame—details she'd never shared with another—and it hadn't repelled him. He'd offered understanding, not recriminations. And he believed in her, believed that she'd grown and learnt since then. That meant everything.

He cupped her tear-streaked cheeks, holding her so she couldn't look away from the honesty in his face. 'I don't believe in love at first sight, Lena,' he said firmly. 'Lust—absolutely. But I didn't know that girl properly from just one look. I do now. I know she's more than a beautiful body and flashing eyes and a husky laugh. She's warm and complicated and human. She's made mistakes but she's not afraid to admit to them. She makes me laugh, she makes me wince, she makes me want things I never thought I'd ever want. I love everything about her. About you.'

'But you were angry with me the other night.' She laid out her last, lingering doubt. 'And you stayed away. Three days, Seth.' The worst three days of her life. 'And today you were so cold, you couldn't talk to me.'

'The other night you dumped all that on me and fled. You didn't even give me a chance to try to understand. That hurt more than what you'd actually said. And as I said before, when I'm hurt I feel angry. Too angry to come near you before now. I hid out in Wellington. Came straight to the stadium from the airport today. You couldn't have made it clearer how much you didn't want me there. But you were as hurt as I was.'

'Oh, Seth.' With shaking hands she clutched his wrists. 'Please tell me this is real.'

He bent and kissed her tenderly. 'Does it feel real?'

'I'm not sure.'

He kissed her again. 'Now?'

She couldn't answer.

'I'm thinking you might need quite some convincing.' He smiled. The old intense, focused, incredible smile.

She smiled, too—as belief, relief and love hummed between them. The kiss this time wasn't gentle. It was passionate and perfect. It had been so long since she'd held him. And she'd never held him like this—not so freely, not so able to let all her feeling for him flow through her fingers. It was sublime. Not just the blaze of lust but the brilliance of unconditional, enduring love.

She broke from it, bursting to tell him. 'I love you.'

He brushed back her hair, his gaze unwavering and true and his smile tender. 'You've told me that before.'

Slowly she nodded. 'I know. But I'm wide awake this time.'

'Me, too. I've been waiting for ages for you to tell me again. To tell me you mean it.'

'I do.' She threw her arms around his neck, desperation incarnate. But it was a delicious, mutual desperation.

It took nothing for him to scoop her into his arms and carry her to her door. Nothing for him to unlock her flat, nothing for him to sweep her dress from her body, his jeans from his.

But it took everything she had to accept how much he loved her. How truly. She felt it all—in the heated strokes of his shaking hands, in the fevered whispers of his hoarse voice, in the powerful demand of his big body.

In this other world, for the first time, Lena felt treasured, beautiful, adored—inside and out. She arched, her mouth sealed to his, giving and receiving so much—extreme pleasure and pure love. She loved him back—loved him with every cell in her body, with the light of her soul. This charming, gorgeous, strong man had taken her, he'd understood her, he'd accepted her. And he'd fulfilled her.

He rolled, lifting her above him so his solid chest cushioned her. 'That day at the stadium I took one look at you and...'

'Wanted to have sex.' She couldn't resist teasing him, loving it more now she felt the truth of his love.

'Well, yeah, but there was something else I wanted just as much.'

'What?'

'You were laughing. You were leaning against that wall and you were laughing so hard and it was so husky and feminine and gorgeous. And my heart just...' He pressed his clenched fist to his chest. 'I've been trying to get you to laugh like that ever since. Don't hide your fun, Lena, be naughty with me. Be tart, be funny. When you laugh, it alters my reality, all for the better. I want that warmth.' He brushed his lips over hers. 'That's what you are to me. Warmth and light and loving.'

How could she not cry then?

He cradled her, gently touching the plaster on her forehead. 'First time in my life I regretted not going to medical school. I wanted to fix that myself. Didn't want a mark left on your beautiful face. Wanted to take care of you so badly. And you wouldn't even talk to me.'

'I was scared. And sad.'

'I'm scared, too, Lena. You were right about lots of things. About my being selfish. About my half-brother.'

Lena raised her head to look into his sombre eyes, to get closer to hear his almost inaudible words.

'I read the letter. He's miserable.'

'Are you going to get in touch?'

'For all the good it might do.' He nodded very slightly.

She cupped the side of his face, feeling his strong jaw, the warmth of his roughened skin. 'It might do a lot.'

His smile was crooked. 'I need your support, Lena. For all my never-fails in the business world, my relationships have been total fails. Every single one. I couldn't bear to make you miserable like Mum and Dad made each other miserable.'

'That would only happen if you left me.'

'Well, that's never happening.' He shuffled down the bed so he brought his eyes level with hers. 'You need certainty and security, Lena. And so do I. I need it a lot. I believe in you and I believe in us. While I've never believed that long-term commitment could work, in my heart I know it'll work with you. I want you to marry me.'

She was shaking her head before he'd finished speaking. 'You never wanted to marry.'

'You were right on that, too. I needed to meet the one woman who'd sink those rubbish ideas of mine. It's you, Lena. It's you. I don't want to be alone any more. I want to be with you.' He pressed his mouth to her neck briefly. 'And you know you're not leaving this bed until you agree to marry me.'

She gazed at the intense, focused expression in his blue eyes and felt her thread of wickedness tighten.

He saw. He smiled.

So did she.

'Going to be a good challenge,' he murmured.

'Oh, yes.' Her laugh came husky and free. Because Lena agreed to it all. 'Yes, yes, yes.'

\* \* \* \* \*

# SEPTEMBER 2011
# HARDBACK TITLES

## ROMANCE

| | |
|---|---|
| The Kanellis Scandal | Michelle Reid |
| Monarch of the Sands | Sharon Kendrick |
| One Night in the Orient | Robyn Donald |
| His Poor Little Rich Girl | Melanie Milburne |
| The Sultan's Choice | Abby Green |
| The Return of the Stranger | Kate Walker |
| Girl in the Bedouin Tent | Annie West |
| Once Touched, Never Forgotten | Natasha Tate |
| Nice Girls Finish Last | Natalie Anderson |
| The Italian Next Door... | Anna Cleary |
| From Daredevil to Devoted Daddy | Barbara McMahon |
| Little Cowgirl Needs a Mum | Patricia Thayer |
| To Wed a Rancher | Myrna Mackenzie |
| Once Upon a Time in Tarrula | Jennie Adams |
| The Secret Princess | Jessica Hart |
| Blind Date Rivals | Nina Harrington |
| Cort Mason – Dr Delectable | Carol Marinelli |
| Survival Guide to Dating Your Boss | Fiona McArthur |

## HISTORICAL

| | |
|---|---|
| The Lady Gambles | Carole Mortimer |
| Lady Rosabella's Ruse | Ann Lethbridge |
| The Viscount's Scandalous Return | Anne Ashley |
| The Viking's Touch | Joanna Fulford |

## MEDICAL ROMANCE™

| | |
|---|---|
| Return of the Maverick | Sue MacKay |
| It Started with a Pregnancy | Scarlet Wilson |
| Italian Doctor, No Strings Attached | Kate Hardy |
| Miracle Times Two | Josie Metcalfe |

MILLS & BOON

# SEPTEMBER 2011
# LARGE PRINT TITLES

## ROMANCE

| | |
|---|---|
| Too Proud to be Bought | Sharon Kendrick |
| A Dark Sicilian Secret | Jane Porter |
| Prince of Scandal | Annie West |
| The Beautiful Widow | Helen Brooks |
| Rancher's Twins: Mum Needed | Barbara Hannay |
| The Baby Project | Susan Meier |
| Second Chance Baby | Susan Meier |
| Her Moment in the Spotlight | Nina Harrington |

## HISTORICAL

| | |
|---|---|
| More Than a Mistress | Ann Lethbridge |
| The Return of Lord Conistone | Lucy Ashford |
| Sir Ashley's Mettlesome Match | Mary Nichols |
| The Conqueror's Lady | Terri Brisbin |

## MEDICAL ROMANCE™

| | |
|---|---|
| Summer Seaside Wedding | Abigail Gordon |
| Reunited: A Miracle Marriage | Judy Campbell |
| The Man with the Locked Away Heart | Melanie Milburne |
| Socialite...or Nurse in a Million? | Molly Evans |
| St Piran's: The Brooding Heart Surgeon | Alison Roberts |
| Playboy Doctor to Doting Dad | Sue MacKay |

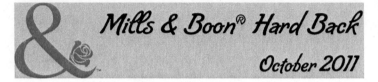

# ROMANCE

| | |
|---|---|
| **The Most Coveted Prize** | Penny Jordan |
| **The Costarella Conquest** | Emma Darcy |
| **The Night that Changed Everything** | Anne McAllister |
| **Craving the Forbidden** | India Grey |
| **The Lost Wife** | Maggie Cox |
| **Heiress Behind the Headlines** | Caitlin Crews |
| **Weight of the Crown** | Christina Hollis |
| **Innocent in the Ivory Tower** | Lucy Ellis |
| **Flirting With Intent** | Kelly Hunter |
| **A Moment on the Lips** | Kate Hardy |
| **Her Italian Soldier** | Rebecca Winters |
| **The Lonesome Rancher** | Patricia Thayer |
| **Nikki and the Lone Wolf** | Marion Lennox |
| **Mardie and the City Surgeon** | Marion Lennox |
| **Bridesmaid Says, 'I Do!'** | Barbara Hannay |
| **The Princess Test** | Shirley Jump |
| **Breaking Her No-Dates Rule** | Emily Forbes |
| **Waking Up With Dr Off-Limits** | Amy Andrews |

# HISTORICAL

| | |
|---|---|
| **The Lady Forfeits** | Carole Mortimer |
| **Valiant Soldier, Beautiful Enemy** | Diane Gaston |
| **Winning the War Hero's Heart** | Mary Nichols |
| **Hostage Bride** | Anne Herries |

# MEDICAL ROMANCE™

| | |
|---|---|
| **Tempted by Dr Daisy** | Caroline Anderson |
| **The Fiancée He Can't Forget** | Caroline Anderson |
| **A Cotswold Christmas Bride** | Joanna Neil |
| **All She Wants For Christmas** | Annie Claydon |

*Mills & Boon® Large Print*

*October 2011*

# ROMANCE

| | |
|---|---|
| **Passion and the Prince** | Penny Jordan |
| **For Duty's Sake** | Lucy Monroe |
| **Alessandro's Prize** | Helen Bianchin |
| **Mr and Mischief** | Kate Hewitt |
| **Her Desert Prince** | Rebecca Winters |
| **The Boss's Surprise Son** | Teresa Carpenter |
| **Ordinary Girl in a Tiara** | Jessica Hart |
| **Tempted by Trouble** | Liz Fielding |

# HISTORICAL

| | |
|---|---|
| **Secret Life of a Scandalous Debutante** | Bronwyn Scott |
| **One Illicit Night** | Sophia James |
| **The Governess and the Sheikh** | Marguerite Kaye |
| **Pirate's Daughter, Rebel Wife** | June Francis |

# MEDICAL ROMANCE™

| | |
|---|---|
| **Taming Dr Tempest** | Meredith Webber |
| **The Doctor and the Debutante** | Anne Fraser |
| **The Honourable Maverick** | Alison Roberts |
| **The Unsung Hero** | Alison Roberts |
| **St Piran's: The Fireman and Nurse Loveday** | Kate Hardy |
| **From Brooding Boss to Adoring Dad** | Dianne Drake |

0911 GEN STD LP

*Discover Pure Reading Pleasure with*

## Visit the Mills & Boon website for all the latest in romance

**Buy** all the latest releases, backlist and eBooks

**Find out** more about our authors and their books

**Join** our community and chat to authors and other readers

**Free** online reads from your favourite authors

**Win** with our fantastic online competitions

**Sign** up for our free monthly eNewsletter

**Tell us** what you think by signing up to our reader panel

**Rate** and review books with our star system

# www.millsandboon.co.uk

 Follow us at twitter.com/millsandboonuk

Become a fan at facebook.com/romancehq